Witchin' Weren't Snowed In

Jenna Collett

Copyright © 2024 by Jenna Collett

All rights reserved.

No part of this publication may be reproduced, distributed, or transmitted in any form or by any means, including photocopying, recording, or other electronic or mechanical methods, without the prior written permission of the publisher, except as permitted by U.S. copyright law.

The story, all names, characters, and incidents portrayed in this production are fictitious. No identification with actual persons (living or deceased), places, buildings, and products is intended or should be inferred.

Book Cover by Jenna Collett

V1

Contents

Chapter 1	1
Chapter 2	12
Chapter 3	25
Chapter 4	35
Chapter 5	45
Chapter 6	54
Chapter 7	64
Chapter 8	73
Chapter 9	82
Chapter 10	92
Chapter 11	109
Chapter 12	116
Chapter 13	121
Chapter 14	132

Chapter 15	145
Chapter 16	158
Epilogue	167
Books Also by	171

Chapter 1
Sage

The meteorologist looked into the camera and scratched the back of his head. His normally chipper tone was thick with confusion. "Well folks, what can I say? Mother Nature can be unpredictable, and the storm we experienced earlier today came out of nowhere." He coughed and cleared his throat, then scraped a hand over his paisley tie. "It's been a wild November so far with record snow totals."

I winced as a chart of historical data filled the screen and waved away the approaching waiter so I could keep watching the news on my phone. The man veered to the next table with his giant tray of shrimp, making my stomach growl in protest. Unfortunately, the shrimp had to wait.

This was bad. *Real bad.* Graphs didn't lie. But the unusual forecast wasn't proof the accumulating snow was my fault. There were plenty of reasons for the sudden storm and none of them had to do with my family's magic. Though I had to admit, if you paired our history with past weather trends, that graph would be awful telling.

The most recent event can be traced back to my cousin Tif. She claimed responsibility for a seasonal drought following her cursed journey through the wonders of online dating. Her experience gave new meaning to the term dry spell.

There have been other occurrences with various relatives—a hail storm here, and a windstorm there. However, it all started with a torrential rainstorm after my great-grandmother was accused of using witchcraft during the highly competitive flower show at her hometown's spring festival.

She literally rained on their parade.

Not intentionally, of course. The weather manifested itself based on her emotions. Which was why I suspected the surprise snowstorm blanketing the city was a coincidence.

Because I was *fine*.

No, not just fine, *fantastic*.

After years of hustling, I was one of the top agents at my office, dedicated to granting holiday miracles and seasonal wonders. Think festive matchmaking and the oddly frequent need to save Christmas—an epidemic, if you asked me—but it made for good job security.

So far, I'd saved historical landmarks from evil conglomerates, planned my share of holiday festivals, and even saved a reindeer. *No, it wasn't one of Santa's, but the ones in the zoo are waiting for their shot.*

Thanks to my high completion rate and the secret intel I'd gathered from the office rumor mill, tonight, I would become the youngest agent to receive corporate's most coveted award: Agent of the Year.

Assuming no one questioned my last case. And possibly the one before that. The reviews were still out on those.

But again, I was *fine.*

I mean fantastic.

"Here's your drink!" My best friend Delia singsonged as she shimmied over to our table carrying a stemmed glass filled with red wine and a frosty cocktail.

I closed the weather forecast on my phone and forced a smile before I collected my glass of wine. Soft music and the hum of conversation flowed around us in the whimsically decorated lounge. The party planning committee had outdone themselves this year.

Twinkling lights were strung throughout the room, giving off a magical glow, while colorful faux leaves hung from invisible wire as if falling from above. In the corner, a fountain spilled sticky caramel alongside a tray of apple spears, and next to it, a massive charcuterie board had been ravaged.

Somewhere, the shrimp cocktail guy still roamed.

Tonight's party was the kickoff to the agency's busy season. Even though our main headquarters was based in the city, many of us were spread out, working remotely, or constantly on travel. This was a chance to gather, be rewarded for our hard work, and allow us to let off some steam before we delved into our latest cases.

No—I would not be hitting the dance floor. I was still living with the vivid memory of my first kickoff party. A fever dream of too many shots and a cringeworthy attempt at the Macarena that led to a wardrobe malfunction thanks to an overzealous hip shake.

The video evidence I'd had erased. Memories, those lasted forever.

Delia leaned her elbows against our high-top table and sipped her cocktail through a tiny straw. She eyed my phone before I tucked it out of view.

"Are you watching the weather again? At a party? I hate to break it to you, but the guy from the news is going to get fired unless you figure out how to stop the snow. It's the third storm this week." Delia smirked. "Have you tried unclenching?"

"I don't need to unclench," I said through ironically clenched teeth. Relaxing my jaw, I plucked a bacon-wrapped scallop from my appetizer plate and chewed, letting the savory bite distract me from Delia's unsolicited attempt at humor. My gaze slid to the bank of windows, granting a panoramic view of the city. Flurries from the earlier storm still floated in the air. "*That* is not because of me."

Delia shrugged. "I'm not convinced. My psychic said your aura felt off when we saw her last week. She said, and I quote, 'A storm is coming, and you can't run from it.' That is seriously cryptic."

"It's called a cold reading, Del! It's a high-probability guess. The "storm" could be anything. I'm never letting you drag me to another fortune teller," I grumbled.

The last thing I needed was mystical wisdom. The woman had taken one look at me and acted as if my presumptive weather curse might be catchy. I'd been tempted to fake a sneeze on her crystal ball, but I didn't want to get my best friend banned from future readings.

Delia pinned me with a knowing stare. The kind she liked to deliver before dropping a truth bomb. I balled up a cocktail napkin, wondering if there was time to grab my plate and make a dash out of the blast radius. Maybe I could still track down the shrimp guy and drown my doubts in cocktail sauce.

"Admit it, Sage." Delia lowered her voice to a murmur. "You're off your game. Last month, you fell asleep while playing matchmaker to a couple of horror buffs on Halloween. You were inside a haunted house. Next to a chainsaw-wielding villain." She shook her head. "Who does that? There's so much screaming."

There had been a lot of screaming. Not that it had helped. One moment I was lying in wait for my targets inside an open coffin, surrounded by waves of magical fog, and the next, lights out. I blamed the dreamlike mist and the oddly comfortable coffin. Delia blamed my constant caseload.

"First off," I said, glancing at the neighboring table to make sure my coworkers weren't eavesdropping. "I swore you to secrecy about that case. Second, I wasn't sleeping. Yes, my eyes were closed for a couple of minutes. But it worked out all right. The chainsaw guy jumped out of the shadows with the assist. My couple will probably invite him to the wedding. They'll even create a mini chainsaw replica to use as a cake topper. Once I got them inside the haunted house, my participation was supervisory at best."

I lifted my wineglass and clinked it into her cocktail before taking a confident sip, certain I'd proved my point.

"Okay, then what about the Fourth of July incident?"

The wine went down the wrong way, and I coughed, sending droplets of Merlot onto the white table linen. "We don't talk about the Fourth of July incident."

Delia sighed and moved my appetizer plate to hide the wet stain. "Sage, you're the best agent in our office. Everyone knows that. You give perfection a run for its money. And one day, if upper management ever gives me a shot at my own case, I want to be just like you."

"No, you don't."

"Well, like you, but with way more work-life balance. And better dance moves."

I wrinkled my nose in disgust. *Will memories ever fade?*

"Speaking of work-life balance, how's your office crush on Simon Delacour coming along? Have you spoken to him?"

Delia couldn't resist glancing at the object of her affection holding court by the bar. There were two things she wanted most this Christmas: a promotion to agent, and a date with Simon. Delia's judgmental fortune teller seemed to think both love and money were in the cards—and I hoped it was—but I still didn't trust that woman.

Looking away, Delia blushed and bent to sip her cocktail until the ice rattled.

"You mean have I spoken to him outside of my head? No. But the two of us had a very witty exchange that I practiced in front of the bathroom mirror this morning. So it's only a matter of time until I graduate to mimicking a conversation with the potted plants in the breakroom."

I stifled a laugh. "You're a study in emotional growth."

"At least I have an emotional well! You bury yourself in casework and avoid anything personal. When was the last time you went on a date? And playing a matchmaker for someone else doesn't count."

She had me there. But I didn't have time for dating. Top agents didn't slow down, they pushed harder. Nose to the grindstone. You'll sleep when you're dead—or conveniently inside a haunted house prop.

"I don't need to find love because I already love my job." I drained my glass and popped the last scallop into my mouth with a grin.

"That's gross, Sage. Do you know who also spent all their time working and ended up alone and unloved around the holidays? Scrooge. Let me be a little Ghost of Christmas Present for you and tell you to get a life. Preferably one with some good kissing."

I faked a gasp and grabbed my purse. "How dare you use Dickens against me? I'm getting us another round before you're possessed by any more ghosts."

As I weaved through the crowd toward the bar, other agents paused in their conversations, giving me a thumbs up or a secret smile. This was my year! I could feel it. Once I reached the top, everything else would fall into place, and I'd finally have the life and recognition I'd always wanted.

Delia was being ridiculous. Though, she might be right about the good kissing part—it had been way too long since I'd experienced any of that. But love? No, thank you. I'd leave that to the couples in my case files.

"Excuse me, Ms. Bennett? May I have a moment of your time?"

The no-nonsense question stopped me in my tracks. Joan, from human resources, waited by the nearly empty cheese display.

She wasn't dressed for the party and still wore her agency badge clipped to the pocket of her fitted blazer. Joan crooked her finger, and my shoulders slumped. Had news of my Halloween nap reached her desk? Getting summoned by human resources after hours was never good.

I nodded and watched longingly as the crowd gathered around the dance floor. They were about to announce this year's award winner. But instead of following them, Joan clasped her hands together and frowned, waiting until I'd joined her.

"Sage, I realize this is a terrible time to have this discussion, but after today's events, it couldn't wait until Monday. It's come to our attention..."

I tuned out Joan's voice and watched over her shoulder as the head of the holiday division picked up the microphone. The festive music went silent when she cleared her throat and began her welcome speech. Next came the big announcement. I held my breath as she presented the award.

"And this season's Agent of the Year award goes to—"

"Ahem, Ms. Bennett? Did you hear me?" Joan waved her hand in front of my face. I blinked, hearing my name, but it wasn't through the microphone. A cheer rang through the crowd as Delia's crush, Simon Delacour, shook hands with the division head before lifting the award trophy into the air.

I'd lost.

But I wasn't supposed to lose.

Something inside me cracked. The applause rose like a gust of wind whipping through the lounge and rushed past my ears. I blinked again. No, the noise wasn't coming from inside. I looked toward the windows where giant flakes mixed with sleet pelted the glass.

I inhaled a shaky breath. The storm had started again, and this time, I couldn't deny it. We weren't dealing with strange weather patterns; we were dealing with magic.

My magic.

Joan rested a hand on my arm and ushered me toward the coatroom. I trailed behind her in a daze. The sound of the wind and the cheerful party grew muffled by the cocoon of thick winter coats. But the coats did nothing to soften the voice in my head.

They didn't wish you good luck; they were laughing at you. Nothing's changed. You haven't changed.

I fixed my watery stare on my dress shoes, then glanced at Joan's red pumps, trying to block the memories from my past I'd tried so hard to leave behind. The lump in my throat refused to budge.

"As I was saying," Joan continued. "After a thorough review of your employee file, including relevant background information, upper management has initiated what we call Operation Merry Reset."

My brow creased at the unfamiliar term. I gave up shoe-watching and asked hopefully, "Is that some form of promotion? Does it come with a plaque?"

"No. It's listed in the handbook. Chapter twenty-six, Section 4, Paragraph 2.6. To summarize, it's when one of our agents enters burnout and is offered the chance for a reset."

A harsh laugh burst from my throat. "But I'm not burned out. I promise! If this is about Halloween, or—" I coughed into my fist. "The Fourth of July—"

"It's about the snow," Joan interrupted. "Well, it's about those other things too, but specifically the snow. We know about your family history, and we can't have our agents manifesting uncontrollable blizzards when they're meant to cast a gentle snowfall to enhance the holiday season. A white Christmas is one thing. Downed power lines, treacherous roads, and postponed festivities are another. It's better if we address the issue before we have to—" Joan leaned in and whispered, "Cancel Christmas."

I barely suppressed a groan. *How original.* This year, someone needed to save Christmas from me.

The agency was overreacting. It was just a little snow! Yes—three unpredictable storms in a week were unusual, but I was sure I could fix it without having to reset, or whatever phrase the agency used in the handbook.

Joan snapped her fingers, and a white envelope with the agency emblem stamped on the front appeared in her hand. She offered it to me with a practiced smile.

"What is that?" I eyed the envelope as if it might give me frostbite.

"Inside is a one-way ticket to the hometown listed in your employee file. We've verified the address with your family and informed them of your arrival."

I froze, feeling like Joan had dunked me in the caramel fountain. "You told my parents I'm coming home for the holidays?"

I hadn't been home in years. Not since I'd left town humiliated and desperate for a fresh start in the city.

Joan pressed the envelope into my hand.

"Your length of stay is based on the successful completion of the terms listed inside your reset paperwork. Please turn in your badge and company laptop to security before you leave." She wagged her finger. "No official casework allowed until you're cleared. It's a liability, and we take these things very seriously."

I nodded, still reeling from the turn of events.

Done with her presentation, Joan tugged on the ends of her blazer and readjusted the badge clipped to her pocket. She gestured toward the door.

"Ms. Bennett, the agency, and myself want to wish you a very merry reset, and best of luck!"

Chapter 2

Sage

Welcome to Cold Spell Mountain.

The taxi drove past the painted welcome sign and into the quaint, snow-swept village. It rolled to a stop outside my family's tea shop and waited with the meter running while I sat in the backseat and checked my email. I held up my phone, grinding my teeth as the picturesque mountains diminished the signal.

A single bar appeared, and I refreshed the screen.

No new messages.

I scowled at my empty inbox. My calendar was also a tale of misery thanks to the agency's reset initiative. In two weeks, I was supposed to be on my way to the small town of Wood Pine to work on my next case, but my research file was locked, and if I didn't meet the requirements listed in the handbook, it would be reassigned.

That was *not* happening.

I'd never had a case reassigned, and I wasn't about to start now. I planned to fix my frozen curse as fast as possible and high-tail it back to the office to reclaim my position before someone else filled it. Because if I didn't, I'd be stuck—unemployed—living my own personal *Groundhog Day* with my past lurking around every corner.

An icy wind sailed into the vehicle. The driver flicked on the windshield wipers as fresh snow began to fall. Where there had been sun moments ago, there were now gray clouds gathering over the mountaintops. I winced, remembering too late I needed to control my emotions.

Outside the vehicle, flakes danced in the air, circling the wrought iron streetlamps and whizzing past brightly colored houses. If the snow had followed me here, the glistening rooftops and slush-covered cobblestone would keep my secret. At least for a little while.

It was a good thing I grew up in ski country and not in Florida. However, I would have given anything to trade in my parka for a swimsuit to avoid my impending family reunion.

Cold Spell might look like it had been plucked straight out of a holiday movie, but for me, the memories lurking here were less heartwarming and felt more like breaking one of my mother's one-of-a-kind teacups—shameful, and no matter how hard you try, impossible to fix.

I eyed the single-story cottage that famously served the best high tea in town. A closed sign hung on the door with a little clock, reminding visitors to come back for their first seating around lunchtime. In the window, tea cups dangled from beaded strings, and cling-on snowflakes dotted the glass. Next to the shop and separated by a narrow alley was my parents' small chalet.

It all looked exactly the same. A picture-perfect postcard that I would have preferred had gotten lost in the mail.

"Are you getting out, lady? I have an early pickup at the lodge."

The driver met my gaze in the rearview mirror, and I almost offered to pay him double to take me back to the airport. Instead, I pulled down my ski hat and grabbed my luggage before climbing out of the vehicle. Buried inside my thick parka, I wheeled my bag across the frozen sidewalk, hoping to be as inconspicuous as possible.

A couple passed by with their morning coffee, and I waved meekly, perched on the stone step in front of my parents' house. First, I rang the bell. Then knocked. So much for the welcoming party. No one was even home. After a call that went straight to my mother's voicemail, I tried the door handle without any luck and cursed myself for losing track of my key.

My parents were notoriously social and could be anywhere in town. But thankfully, I knew where they kept a spare key.

I glanced next door, then down the alley leading to the back of the shop. The cottage windows were old, and one had a loose latch. If you maneuvered it just right, you could unlock it from the outside.

It didn't open far thanks to the worn casing, so my parents had never bothered to fix it. That, and crime in town was rare—besides, who in their right mind wanted to steal mismatched tea cups? I could be in and out, huddled under the covers in my old bedroom within minutes, or spend hours sitting in a busy coffee shop, trying to avoid familiar faces.

Breaking and entering for the win!

Leaving my luggage on the stoop, I walked to the back of the shop and found the window with the loose latch. Even though it didn't face the street, the window casing was covered in a festive garland of pine needles and twinkling lights. My mother always believed it was as important to decorate the places people didn't see as the ones they do.

I moved some pallets underneath to give me more height, then peered through the glass. Morning light spilled over the stainless steel counters and illuminated the hanging racks of pots and pans.

From where I stood, I glimpsed the spare key hanging on a hook by a shelf of tea canisters. I removed my mittens and rubbed my hands together for warmth—okay, mostly courage. Was it still trespassing if your parents owned the place? The town might be low on crime, but leave it to me to commit a misdemeanor. With the luck I was having, I'd spend the holiday in handcuffs.

Bracing myself against the window, I wriggled the panes until the latch fell out of place, then put my shoulder into opening it as far as it would go. The casing screeched in protest and pine needles from the garland tickled my nose.

I tapped my boot on the wooden pallet, studying the gap in the window. I thought it would be wider. Then again, I also thought there'd be a banner outside the house celebrating my homecoming.

Looking over my shoulder, I made sure the alley was clear, then hoisted myself through the window. I grunted as my body contorted into a pretzel on the narrow windowsill and teetered precariously over the countertop. Regrets? I had a few—mostly my aversion to the gym and the idea I had any sort of balance. Window gymnastics was meant for people who regularly went to yoga.

And people wearing a less bulky coat.

Just as I made the transition to the other side of the window, my jacket snagged on a nail holding the garland. My momentum sent me reeling as the fabric ripped, and I toppled like one of those flying squirrels onto the counter. A flour canister tipped over in my wake and a poof of flour filled the air.

Ironically, the puffy coat that triggered the fall aided in the landing. Who knew sportswear was such a double-edged sword?

"Oh, come on!" I groaned as I inhaled a faceful of flour. The fine dust settled around me like one of my magical snowstorms—both of which were making my life miserable.

Happy homecoming, Sage Bennett! This relaxation retreat is really working.

The sound of footsteps creaked in the other room.

I lifted my head; unease tossing ice water on the hot flames of my indignity.

"Mom? Dad? I'm in the kitchen. Can I get some help?"

The footsteps paused, and when no one answered, a weird feeling skated up my spine. In the past, we'd had run-ins with local kids playing pranks on our family. Well—me mostly.

They only played pranks on me. Stupid stuff like putting a frog in my backpack at school, and once while I was working in the shop, someone slipped food coloring into all the teapots, turning everyone's tea green.

But that was years ago, and no one in town knew I'd arrived. Which meant the intruder on the other side of the kitchen door wasn't here to embarrass me. My heart pounded as the footsteps resumed, moving rapidly toward the kitchen.

I barely had time to react, let alone get off the flour-covered counter. Frantic, I slid my hands in front of me, blindly searching for something to use as a weapon.

"Don't come any closer! I swear, if this is another prank—"

The door swung open as I grasped a metal object and brandished it in front of my face. The rest of my threat died on my lips.

There he stood.

Because, of course, it wasn't my parents, or a robber, or even a heroic firefighter who'd heard the commotion and rushed over to help. Now there was a rescue I could get behind. But no. It was the only person from my past I'd hoped I wouldn't run into.

Leo Grayson.

Did people have arch-rivals or was that just a fictional villain in the movies? Either way, in the movie of my life, Leo was the enemy.

Growing up, he'd had a perfect life: he'd been a popular ski instructor at the local resort, came from a wealthy family that vacationed overseas, and had looks that made me suspect he modeled for a winter sports catalog in his downtime.

He still had the looks, by the way—tall and athletic from years spent on the ski slopes. Dark, tousled hair, and rough stubble that chipped away at his clean-cut persona. And those eyes—brown like gingerbread and so expressive, they pulled you in until your insides felt like warm molasses.

We all have one person who we hope ages poorly; Leo did not get the memo.

But none of that was his fault, and I could have overlooked all of it if only he hadn't broken my heart.

"Sage?" Leo's voice was a mix of amusement and surprise. "It's been a long time. I can't tell if you're trying to bake me cookies or planning to whisk me to death?"

What? I focused on my makeshift weapon. Crap, I'd grabbed a whisk. I thought I'd met my humiliation quota as a teenager, but apparently, there was a whole other level involving kitchen utensils.

"It's the second one," I said, dropping the whisk onto the counter to push myself to a seated position.

Leo laughed, and the sound made my insides twist. I hated that something as normal as a laugh affected me so much.

"Are you okay?" he asked, struggling to keep a concerned expression on his face.

I wiped at my cheeks and tried to blink away the flour dust. "Do I look okay? I ripped my coat and there's flour everywhere!"

"Hold on. You're making it worse. Let me help." Leo grabbed a cloth and ran it under the faucet. "May I?" he asked, holding the dish towel.

If I was smart, I'd bolt back to the house and try to forget this window caper ever happened. There was probably enough spiked eggnog in my mother's fridge to give someone a case of amnesia. But I couldn't stop the questions swirling in my mind.

"Fine." I scooted back an inch when Leo flattened a palm on the counter and leaned in, keeping me from running off. Were my thoughts tattooed on my forehead?

"What are you doing in the tea shop?" I asked, trying to distract myself as he carefully wiped away the flour on my cheeks. Not that my question helped. Leo's clean, citrusy scent was doing a number on my senses. I cleared my throat and angled my chin. "Better yet, what are you doing in Cold Spell? I thought you were living the dream at some swanky ski resort in France."

"Stalking my socials, Bennett?"

"I'd rather get hit in the face with a snowball, Grayson."

The corner of Leo's mouth curved, and my throat constricted when he reached up to adjust my ski hat, brushing flour from there too. Static snapped between us. His fingers tangled gently in my hair, pushing the wayward strands off my face.

It was too hot in this kitchen. Between my double-insulated parka, my ski hat, and Leo's proximity, I needed a blast of cold air. A snowball to the face wasn't an exaggeration, it was an invitation.

"Look, I don't know what you're doing here, but you should leave before I call the cops." I pushed off the counter, forcing Leo to step back. He slung his arms across his chest and cocked his head. My threat didn't seem to have an effect.

"How long are you staying?" he asked.

"That is none of your business." I swept past him, flicking my wrist to send a magical gust of air toward the flour on the counter that sent the dust sailing into the sink. The rest, I'd have to come back and clean up later.

I grabbed the spare key off the hook, pressing it into my palm until it hurt. Avoiding conflict was straight out of Old Sage's playbook. New Sage was casting emotional blizzards and wanted an explanation.

"You know what? I'm not leaving until you answer my question. What are you doing here?"

Before he could speak, the front door to the tea shop opened with a jingle, and I heard my parents' laughter as they came inside. Leo's gaze held mine in a standoff as he pushed the swinging door open and shouted, "We're in here, Suzanne and David!"

Suzanne and David? Since when did Leo call my parents by their first names? Things were getting weirder by the minute.

"Look who's finally home!" my mother cried as she entered the kitchen. "Get over here and give me a hug."

My father walked in behind her, and as my mother pulled me into a perfume-drenched hug, he clapped Leo on the back and gave me a wide grin. "There's our big city girl!"

"Hey, Dad." Wasn't anyone concerned about Leo's intrusion? Apparently not. My mother ended the hug and held me at arm's length. Her brows drew together as she plucked the hat off my head.

"Oh, sweetie, what did you do to your hair?"

"What do you mean?" I self-consciously touched the smooth strands that ended near my collarbone. It was a new style, and I'd woken up extra early before my flight to make sure it was perfect.

My mother clucked her tongue with disappointment. "Your hair used to be full of life. Now it just hangs there."

I reached for my hat and resisted the urge to put it back on. I twisted the wool between my fingers and swallowed hard. "What you call life was frizz, Mom. This is better."

"I guess that's how you gals wear it in the city," she said, pressing her lips together in a thin line.

"It's how anyone who knows how to work a hot iron wears it," I mumbled, glancing at Leo.

My cheeks burned. When I was younger, my long, frizzy hair was the bane of my existence. Nothing seemed to tame it. Sage the Frizzy Mage became a schoolwide nickname and my classmates would toss crumpled paper at me in the halls to see if they could make the pieces stick.

All I saw was pity in Leo's eyes. I looked away, trying to re-bottle my emotions. Unfortunately, that's when I spotted the wall.

I extracted myself from my mother's scrutiny and walked in horror toward the large corkboard of photos hanging near the pantry.

"What is this?" I asked, grazing a finger over a picture of myself sipping a fruity cocktail under a palm tree on the beach. A photo I'd cropped super close to hide the fact the beach was actually a mural at a Caribbean Fusion restaurant in the city. Next to it was a series of shots from the luxury condo Delia and I had toured during an open house. We'd taken turns photographing each other as if we owned the place.

My actual apartment was the size of a shoebox and rumbled daily thanks to its proximity to the transit station.

So much for location, location, location!

There were *so many* photos. Travel shots. Plates of food. Me with the reindeer I rescued.

"Did you print out my Instagram feed?" My mouth fell open as I scanned the corkboard.

Most people's feeds were notoriously embellished. Mine was practically fiction with a warm-toned filter. Even the one with the reindeer—I really did save it!—but they took the picture right before the reindeer sneezed on me and ruined my favorite ugly Christmas sweater. One that oddly featured its long-lost brother with a big red pom-pom.

"We did!" my father crowed. "Isn't technology amazing?" He pointed to an empty spot near the center of the corkboard. "And we saved a space to immortalize your award. We can't wait to get a photo of you holding it. Your mom and I are proud of how much you've achieved at the agency."

"I've already told all my friends at bookclub," my mother chimed in. "Oh, and Susan, who works over at the Cold Spell Gazette, said to send her the photo and she'll feature it in the business section. Can you believe it? A feature! This is the biggest news to hit our town since Mary Higgens' daughter won a walk-on role in a sitcom! I had to hear about it every time I went out to collect the paper. When Mary reads the feature, she'll be green with envy."

"My award?" I choked.

That was the thing about small towns. Everyone knew everyone, and even the smallest news spread faster than icing melting on a hot cookie. The agency might have informed my parents I was coming home, but they hadn't revealed the reason. My parents probably assumed I was on a celebratory vacation.

Hearing the surprise in my voice, my mother's eyes narrowed with suspicion. "You won, Agent of the Year, didn't you? Because in your last email, you said it was a sure thing."

I withered under her critical gaze, and a knot of self-doubt tightened under my rib cage. The truth was a block of ice inside my chest, and I was frozen by the fear of disappointment. I'd worked so hard, but anything other than returning home a success would be considered a failure. I couldn't face those knowing looks.

People faked it till they made it all the time. What was one more fabricated photo when I'd come so close?

"Um...of course, I won Agent of the Year. The award's in my luggage. We can take a photo later."

Assuming I could conjure up a fake trophy.

"I know the perfect place," my mother gushed, wrapping her arm around Leo in a way that made my nose crinkle in disgust. "You can do a photoshoot at Leo's ski lodge. It'll be the perfect backdrop for your photo."

"Wait—Leo owns the lodge? I thought it sold to some obnoxious developer last year, you know, the kind that likes to strip out all the small-town charm and replace it with corporate logos and a soulless experience."

"Sage!" my mother gasped. "Where are your manners? Leo's company purchased the resort, and he's hired our shop to host an afternoon tea. If it goes well, it'll run through the season." Her voice lowered with a warning. "We're partners, so be nice, dear."

My gaze snapped to Leo's and suddenly the reason he'd been lurking around the tea shop became clear. He wasn't in France because he was here, winning over my parents with his manufactured charm and piles of money. The whole town was likely falling at his feet, lauding his acquisition of the rustic resort as if it were the new town jewel and he was their king.

As if mocking my speculation, a gust of wind swept through the open window, catching the whisk I'd left on the counter and rolling it to a stop near Leo's feet—a bad omen if I'd ever seen one.

Leo bent to retrieve the fallen whisk, then held it out to me, offering the utensil as if it were a peace offering, but I knew it was a challenge to a duel. He winked. "Welcome home, partner."

Chapter 3

Leo

If whisks were sharp, I'd be dead.

Sage eyed the utensil between us. An awkward moment passed before she took it from me with a strained smile. One that was mostly for her parents' benefit. She dropped it back onto the counter, then wiped her hand on her coat as if it could wipe away my existence.

Nice try, City Girl.

Though her latest nickname didn't match the Sage I'd known since we were in high school. None of them had ever fit. Because few people knew the real Sage.

Hair changed. Clothes evolved. But Sage's vulnerability, wrapped up with stubbornness and a dash of sharp humor, was bone deep. She had just learned to package it differently.

And I didn't hate it—or the way she'd looked dusted in flour—though it was pretty clear she still hated me. I was lucky she hadn't been able to reach the butcher's block before I walked into the kitchen.

Although, her murderous expression had morphed into one of mortification. Not that I blamed her. Coming face-to-face with your staged selfies on the kitchen wall was rough. It almost made me want to switch my profile to private.

"Well, this has been so much fun, but I should go unpack. I'll let myself into the house." Sage flashed the key in her palm and pulled her ski hat back over her head, hiding her sleek blonde hair. "Wake me up when it's New Year's," she mumbled under her breath before striding toward the swinging kitchen door.

"Wait, honey! You have to join us for lunch at the lodge. We've been so busy there's nothing in the fridge except eggnog, and you know how your father is with the rum ratio."

"Trust me, there's not enough eggnog in Cold Spell," Sage said over her shoulder.

Suzanne trailed behind her, and I could barely make out their hushed conversation by the front door.

"Forget it. I'm not having lunch with him."

"At least try, dear. We need this arrangement," Suzanne whispered. "Your father and I had to use some of our retirement savings to pay off a loan for the shop, and now we're behind."

"Mom, why didn't you—?"

David cleared his throat loud enough to urge Sage and her mother to continue their conversation outside. When the door closed with a soft jingle, he sighed and wiped a hand through his long beard. "My daughter's probably jet-lagged. I'm sure she'll come around. She'll be impressed by what you've done with the place."

Impressed? Try skeptical. Sage would likely start a petition to shut down the resort and kick my commercialized and soulless butt straight out of ski country. The most logical plan was to steer clear of her until she completed her hometown victory lap and went back to her busy life in the city. Because for someone who acted as if he didn't have a care in the world, I was surprisingly risk averse.

Acquiring the lodge had been my first risk, not only financially, but because I'd left the stability of my father's real estate development company and struck out on my own. I couldn't afford to let anything get in the way. But deep down, it was more than that. I needed this place to succeed. I needed its permanence. I'd spent too many years chasing something that had never chased me back.

I wasn't about to let Sage Bennett sweep into town, put my entire world in one of her magical blenders, and hit liquefy.

She'd enjoy it too much.

My phone buzzed, and I checked the notification. Another emergency at the resort. Something about a mechanical issue with the chairlift. The last thing we needed when we were trying to attract guests was skiers stranded in mid-air.

"I have to get back. Let me know if there are any issues with the setup for your event. If you can't reach me, contact my assistant, Valerie."

"Will do!" David lifted a hand in a wave, but paused, noticing the open window and fallen flour canister. He frowned.

"What happened here? Wait—If my daughter was involved, I don't want to know. I'll get a broom."

By the time I'd put on my jacket and exited the tea shop, both Suzanne and Sage were nowhere to be found. I shivered inside my coat as snowflakes pelted me in the face. The weather forecast had predicted sun, but any snow would be good for the slopes and save us from having to run the snow cannons. From a cost standpoint, I'd take all the white fluffy stuff I could get.

Tourist season wasn't in full swing, and the drive to the lodge was short. After Thanksgiving would be the real test to see if the resort could draw in the crowds as it had in the past.

Since securing the property, I'd sunk my own funds into updating structural defects and worked hard to bring the place up to code. So far, it had been nothing but a money pit drenched in rustic charm. But I was counting on that specific brand of charm to pay dividends.

Even sitting beneath storm clouds, the main building was a sight to see. Timber and natural stone framed the floor-to-ceiling windows that overlooked the snow-capped mountains. The resort grounds were dotted with flagstone fire pits and snowshoe trails, and a wraparound deck boasted an oversized hot tub.

Currently, the lodge had twenty-three boutique guest rooms—twenty-two if you didn't count the one I'd been living out of since I arrived back in Cold Spell—and if everything went accordingly; I had plans for expansion.

But first, we needed guests.

The resort had floundered the last few seasons, losing traction to some of the larger, more modern hotels. It also didn't help that we had a tricky public relations issue. Sage wasn't wrong when she accused a developer of stripping the charm from our small town. It just wasn't me.

Two years ago, my father's company brokered a deal that closed one of the town's historical landmarks so he could put in a parking lot. Another deal shuttered the local ice skating rink and the surrounding park. They're building luxury condos there now.

I'd been overseas while my father sacrificed the town's character for profit. When I returned home, I wasn't the most welcome man in Cold Spell.

Scrooge himself would have fared better.

Everyone was waiting for the bulldozers to arrive. They certainly weren't lining up to buy lift tickets or enjoying the newly renovated guest rooms with working fireplaces. I was merely an extension of my father, trying to squeeze the last bit of money out of the lodge before I tore down another cherished landmark.

No one believed I had other intentions. The irony was, I only had one shot at this. I had enough money for this season, and if I failed, the resort would end up on another developer's chopping block.

The snow had tapered off as I climbed the wide stone steps leading into the lodge. Valerie, my assistant, greeted me in the lobby, a two-way radio clipped to her hip and a coffee tumbler clutched in her hand.

She was fresh out of college and the only one I'd interviewed who hadn't blocked my number when they learned the salary. Valerie was also a lifesaver, keeping me organized and on schedule. There wasn't anything she couldn't fix with a spreadsheet and caffeine. Well—except for my current reputation.

"Let me read your schedule for the day," Valerie said, keeping pace with me as we walked through the spacious lobby. "You have a meeting with the contractor in an hour, a wine delivery at noon, and there's a staff meeting at three. I also texted you about the broken chairlift. The mechanic is working on it as we speak."

"Any new reservations?"

Valerie dodged the question and tried to distract me by tossing a freshly baked muffin from our complimentary coffee station in my direction.

"Have you tried one of these yet? They're fantastic. Hiring the Bennetts to provide baked goods from their shop was genius. Now if we could only figure out how to get people in here to eat them." She grabbed a muffin for herself and refilled her tumbler. "By the way, how did you get the Bennetts on our side?"

"They needed the money. I'm sure they attended the town meeting disguised as a Grayson roast, like everyone else."

"Gotcha." Valerie made a sympathetic face.

I leaned against the coffee station and noted the vacant reservation desk on the other side of the lobby. The clerk had his elbows on the counter, playing a game on his phone. At least he wasn't sleeping.

"Do you have that list of influencers? We should start with one of them. Our budget is pretty much non-existent, but we could have them hold another company's product while standing in front of our mountain. We wouldn't have to pay full price for that."

Valerie snickered and scrolled through her phone. "I don't think that's how it works. Nice try, though. Forget influencers for the moment. What you need is a local. Someone who can help you make inroads with the community. We need to change the town's perception of you."

"It can't be that bad. Sure, there's the history with my father, but I grew up here. They know me."

"They *knew* you. A lot of time has passed and recent memories overshadow old ones. Not to freak you out, but the other day, people in line at the grocery store mentioned the word boycott."

I cringed. Boycott was bad.

"Do you know any locals who would work within our pitiful budget? Better yet, for free?" I joked, taking a bite of the muffin. It was delicious. Freshly baked this morning with extra blueberries and a sugar-crusted top. Our rivals used pre-packaged pastries. They definitely didn't source local coffee beans.

"You can't use some of your charisma to find someone?" Valerie teased. "I thought you were once voted most likely to be on the cover of a lifestyle magazine."

The muffin caught in the back of my throat, and I coughed, trying to dislodge it from my windpipe. "Some charisma. I was nearly beaten with a whisk this morning inside the tea shop. I'm not stepping a foot into the hardware store. Too many saws." I sank my teeth into the muffin for another bite, chewing slowly as an idea nagged at me.

Was Sage Bennett's homecoming the answer? She'd gone from a shy introvert who'd been picked on because she was different to a wildly successful career woman. One who happened to work in the miracle department. Because that's what this would take: a miracle.

But no. It would never work. To win over the town, first I'd have to win over her.

With our history, I might as well save myself the trouble, put on a Santa suit, and hand over the deed to the resort as a Christmas gift. I didn't need to go digging around in old wounds that had never healed properly.

Still...

I scrubbed a hand over my face. This resort was worth fighting for. This town was worth fighting for. They just needed to believe I was the man to do it. And there was no denying it. For that, I needed Sage.

"Actually, I might know someone. The Bennetts have a daughter who is back in town. From what they've told me about her job, she has experience handling this type of thing. Supposedly, she works miracles around the holidays, which we seriously need at this point. It's unusual, and I'm sure she'll say no because she hates me, but—"

"Wait, she hates you? I like her already. When can she start?" Valerie wriggled her eyebrows over the rim of her tumbler.

"Remind me again why I hired you?"

"Because I'm smart," she said, using a coffee stirrer to punctuate her point. "And when this place is raking in the tourist money, you're going to give me a raise."

"Don't get ahead of yourself. First, we need to figure out a plan. Sage Bennett won't help save the resort just because I ask nicely. I believe her last words to me before she left town were, 'I never want to see you again.'"

"Ouch. What did you do?"

"It's a long story. One which should have had a different ending, but here we are."

Valerie drummed her fingers on the counter, her manicured nails echoing through the empty lobby. She smiled slowly. The mischief in her eyes made me think I should stick to my idea with the Santa suit.

"Look, I know it's not your fault, but it's common knowledge you're a villain in this town."

"Unjustly!" I scowled, already dreading where her thoughts were headed.

"The plan is simple. We need some leverage. All you have to do is uncover a tiny secret you can use to pressure Sage to help with the resort. Everyone has them. I have them. You have them. It'll work because it's human nature to want to keep those secrets hidden."

"You're diabolical." I tossed the muffin wrapper into the trashcan and shook my head. "I'll find another way. I'm not that desperate."

"You are that desperate. I've seen your accounting. I hate to say it but to save this place, this town—heck, to save Christmas! You're going to have to think like a villain." Valerie propped her hands on her hips and grinned. "And you're in luck because I'll be your festive minion."

Chapter 4
Sage

The sound of jingle bells pierced the morning air, alerting me to check my notifications.

I rolled onto my back, cursing the measly size of my twin bed, and stared at the boy band poster tacked to the ceiling. *Life comes at you fast. One minute, you're at the top of the career ladder, and the next, you're in your childhood bedroom wondering how the cute, blond band leader did with his solo career.*

Heaving a sigh, I reached for my phone.

One new email.

I shoved the covers away and scooted against the pillow. Fingers crossed, it was a cry for help. A pleading missive from the agency begging me to return, or maybe my award had been stuck at the engravers and was on its way here by overnight express. Anything to save me from having to devise a decoy.

My parents had asked to see the trophy at dinner, and I convinced them to wait until I'd organized the photo shoot. Which wasn't happening under any circumstances. There was no way I'd pose in front of a cozy fireplace decorated with pine cones and satin ribbons at Leo's lodge.

Ugh...why was he here? Can't a girl return to her hometown with a bruised ego and a self-care mandate without running into her nemesis?

According to a lifetime of holiday rom-coms, the answer was no. But my job was to facilitate other people's romantic pairings and personal growth, not my own—and considering the way my pairing with Leo had ended, I didn't relish a do-over.

What we had might have burned bright, but it was short-lived, similar to my comical attempt at skiing when my parents forced me to get an outdoor hobby.

That's where I met Leo—the ski instructor assigned to teach beginner lessons. Sure, the group was full of ten-year-olds, and we stayed on the bunny slope, but it turned out to be fun, and I felt comfortable being myself around him.

In school, Leo was the popular jock. But on the slopes, he was different—carefree, funny, patient. He made me laugh and helped me up every time I fell. It didn't take long until I fell for him, too.

We became inseparable, hanging out after my lessons, and for one glorious season, I was secretly in love with my best friend. When he asked me out, I thought he felt the same way too. Until the night of our date, when he never showed. Lucky for me, his friends arrived to witness my humiliation. They laughed and told me Leo was never interested and he'd moved on to someone worth his time. In their eyes, I was still the weird girl—the witch—they made fun of.

Nothing was the same after, and I left town for a new life in the city.

And that's why we don't fall in love with our ski instructors, folks. They'll stab you in the heart with their ski pole.

I shoved the memories away before I could spiral. Leo and I were ancient history. There were skeletons in the Smithsonian who had a better chance of resurrection than our failed romance.

I focused on my phone. Unfortunately, the email wasn't from the agency. It was from Delia.

Just in case you need some help to get started. Attached is an article on self-care. Though, I suppose if you're reading this, you won't like number five: Digital Detox.
It's a doozy.
XOXO Del

I rolled my eyes and clicked to open the article. Scanning the text, I made a note of the ways to reverse burnout, stopping before hitting number five. We weren't touching that one yet. Probably never.

1. Power Naps: *I slept eight hours so I can check that one as done.*

2. Mindful Breathing: *Sounds stressful.*

3. Aromatherapy: *Lavender makes me sneeze.*

4. Walking in Nature: *Are there bears in Cold Spell?*

Dropping my head back, I consulted with the band members on the ceiling. They were noncommittal. I set my jaw and tossed my phone toward the foot of the bed. Stopping the snow was priority number one. It was the only way I'd get my life back on track.

I also had a side quest. Keeping up my assumed picture-perfect life was the key to keeping my past squarely in the past while I was in Cold Spell.

There was also the bonus objective to avoid Leo at all costs.

The two main goals overlapped. So I'd combine them and keep my eyes out for a certain rugged resort owner.

I'd start with walking in nature with the added twist of popping into the antique shop to find something to use as a fake trophy. Then I'd finish with some aromatherapy by way of inhaling a peppermint mocha.

That sounded pretty good. *See!* I could relax.

I was going to break this weather curse so hard, they'd beg me to make it snow.

Storm clouds brewed overhead as I stepped into the tea shop. Guests occupied a few of the linen-draped tables, and the sound of clinking china melded with the flow of pleasant conversation.

The tea shop was one of my favorite places. It was a sweet haven from the bustling streets during tourist season. A spot where you could relax with a cup of tea and try some of my father's famous quiche. I used to settle in the corner with a book after class, escaping into a fantasy world, preferring fiction over my real life. The happy endings didn't come easy, but they never let you down.

My mother walked by carrying a three-tiered dish of finger sandwiches. She deposited it at one of the tables, then recited the list of delicacies, signaling out her favorite: Smoked salmon with cream cheese. Then she placed a small note card on the table.

"What are those?" I asked as she joined me near the door.

"Announcements for our first tea at the lodge. We're trying to get the word out. It's been difficult to drum up interest and we need this partnership with Leo. After everything we went through the last few years with the loan for the tea shop; I never want to experience that again. We almost lost everything."

"I'm sorry, Mom. I didn't know. But it can't be difficult to find people to show up. Everyone in town loves your tea."

My mother gently patted the nape of her neck where she had twisted her hair in a high bun. She leaned in conspiratorially and whispered, "No one wants to come because of the Graysons."

Surprise tinged my voice. "You mean the monarchs of Cold Spell? I'm shocked they haven't changed the town name to Grayson at this point. What do they have to do with it?"

"They've fallen from grace. Didn't you read my last holiday letter? It was all in there."

I nodded even though I had *not* read the letter. My mother's version of a holiday letter was at least twelve pages of handwritten gossip. Even if you deciphered the penmanship, there was a mix of miscellaneous details—like when Donald, from down the street, started painting his front door to match the seasons—to a detailed recounting of the neighborhood watch.

Spoiler alert: It was Ms. Higgens' dog who kept stealing the Cold Spell Gazette from my mother's porch, not a news-obsessed bandit. Case closed.

After that, I skimmed the letters.

But now I wished I hadn't. There was figurative spilled tea in that letter about Leo's family, and I'd missed it!

"Refresh my memory?" I asked, as my father poked his head out of the kitchen and signaled for my mother.

"Sorry dear, I have to help your father with the crumb cake. Are you headed downtown?"

"Yeah. I stopped in to see if you guys needed anything."

"As a matter of fact, we do. Thanksgiving is tomorrow and I haven't had time to get everything for our meal. I'll send you the list." She walked away, then paused, and I hoped for a little taste of the Grayson gossip. "Oh honey, did you see the scarf I left for you by the front door? You should wear it. It was the last thing your great-grandmother knitted for you before she died."

I wrinkled my nose. *Guilt trip much?* But she wasn't finished.

"If you double wrap it and wear your hat, it will hide your hair."

"Goodbye, Mom," I mumbled.

I tried to ignore the dig and stepped outside to find the clouds had darkened and snow fell, coating the sidewalk. Peering into the sky, I blinked away the flakes that stuck to my lashes. I wasn't off to a great start. It didn't help I now had to brave the grocery store right before the holiday.

But everything was fine.

No, fantastic!

My phone jingled with my mother's shopping list, and I brushed the giant flakes off the screen to view the items. It would be better to get the stressful errand out of the way first so I could focus on the walking in nature and aromatherapy mashup I had planned. I'd need the calming boost after—I squinted at the list—I tracked down truffle butter.

Where did one even find truffle butter? If it didn't come in stick form or in one of those plastic tubs, I had no idea.

The snow fell faster, and I inhaled a mindful breath. Then another. It wasn't as stressful as I'd imagined. The flakes eased up, so I straightened my shoulders and marched back to my parent's house to grab the reusable shopping bags.

Out of protest, I did not wear my great-grandmother's scarf.

A short time later, I parked the car in one of the only available spots and hiked through the slushy lot toward the market entrance. Shoppers buzzed in and out of the sliding glass doors, loaded with bags and pushing carts brimming with holiday ingredients.

I grabbed a shopping cart and checked the list again. I would be efficient and organized. I would not get distracted by non-list items. Most importantly, I would not walk down memory lane, no matter who I ran into. *Therein lies the path to chaos...*

"Sage Bennett! Is that you? Wow! It's been ages. Those teenage years are so awkward. Am I right? But you look amazing now and so grown-up."

And...I was just shoved down memory lane. Thankfully, the rocky path was paved with a few scattered compliments. Too bad I'd only made it to the produce aisle.

"Mrs. Thompson! It's good to see you. Are you still teaching ninth-grade science?"

Mrs. Thompson maneuvered her cart to the side, letting another couple slide past. "I'm retired now. No more science fairs for me. Gosh, remember yours? I still have nightmares." She winked. "See what I did there?"

I did. Mrs. Thompson had made a sleep pun.

The thing was, I'd wanted to make a volcano. A perfectly normal and unproblematic project that would get me an A, and also leave me socially unscathed. But my mother insisted I show off the Bennett family mood detection tea. Not mood enhancer—that's a different thing. This was more like a mood ring, but with tea.

The potion had passed from generation to generation, transcribed over the years until it was my mother's turn to write it down. But not unlike the penmanship in her holiday letters, the potion card was unreadable.

I was also going through a phase where I refused to wear my glasses because they were too big for my face. Either way, I mixed up the ingredients, and instead of turning the tea blue when someone was happy; the potion had an unfortunate side effect: drowsiness. Like intense drowsiness. Everyone who drank my tea fell asleep, and we had to stop the fair early.

I did not get an A or leave socially unscathed. That year, my classmates called me Sage the Snoozy Mage and pretended to fall asleep whenever I spoke.

"So tell me," Mrs. Thompson said, leaning on the handle of the cart like she planned to stay awhile. "What does it feel like to win such a prestigious award at the agency? Did they hold a huge banquet?" She pressed a hand against her heart and whispered reverently, "Were you wearing a designer label?"

"Well—"

Mrs. Thompson didn't let me finish. "Your mother told us all about your success at bookclub, and I told everyone at the historical center. Someone even made a flyer and put it on the bulletin board at the post office."

"I hope they didn't use my yearbook photo," I said, trying to disguise my agony.

Only in my hometown would they post my alleged achievement right next to the federal wanted posters. Memory lane had morphed into a dark future alley, and I needed an off-ramp.

"Oh, look—fresh turkeys are half-off! Better grab one before they sell out." I pointed toward the back of the store and when Mrs. Thompson fell for my ruse, I dashed down the cereal aisle.

This town wasn't big enough for me and my emotional baggage, and I still hadn't found anything on my shopping list. Keeping my head low, and my perfectly styled hair in my face—thank goodness for curtain bangs—I managed to locate the truffle butter.

The rest of the list I slowly added to the cart, wheeling between shoppers like I was moving through a maze while memories from my past waited at the end of every aisle. Until I'd reached the coveted cheese case and spotted the most terrifying dead end of them all: Leo Grayson picking out a wheel of brie.

How was it possible for a man to look that good under the harsh fluorescent lighting of the supermarket? It wasn't fair. He was even backlit by a variety of gourmet cheese, and let's face it, life was just better with cheese. If he had a bottle of wine tucked under his arm, I'd melt like fondue in front of the cracker display.

Cleanup on aisle twelve.

I pivoted, nearly knocking over a rack of bagel chips. There would be no sharp cheddar at the Bennett family Thanksgiving this year. A tragic, but necessary sacrifice.

Now I needed to get out of this store without Leo seeing me, or memory lane might turn into memory quicksand, and a discounted turkey wouldn't be enough to pull me out.

Chapter 5

Leo

"I think Sage spotted me." I placed the wheel of brie into the cart.

Valerie tossed a ball of mozzarella beside it and popped the collar of her jacket to hide her face. "She didn't see us. We've been super subtle, and this place is packed."

"Subtle is not wearing oversized sunglasses inside the supermarket. Why are you in disguise? Sage doesn't know who you are." I scraped a hand over my jaw. "I don't know. This whole thing feels weird."

"It's only weird if we make it weird. Besides, aren't you going to some big, fancy Thanksgiving dinner? You can't show up empty-handed. Buy a pie or a cheese board. Now you're shopping for real." Valerie wheeled the cart in the direction Sage had vanished.

I internally groaned and followed. Our supermarket stakeout had been a horrible idea. Not only because you'd have to be a glutton for punishment to step foot near the market so close to Thanksgiving, but also because I still wasn't sold on Valerie's 'think like a villain' plan.

On paper, it was genius, but in the real world, it felt dirty and counterproductive to my goal. I wasn't good at deception or taking advantage. Those were my father's traits.

Traits I knew he wished I embodied. In some twisted form, this plan would endear me to him in a way just being his son never had. Some fathers take their sons fishing, others teach them the art of corporate takeover. Now here I was, using nefarious business tactics to hijack Sage's help.

Apple, say hello to the tree you fell from.

Valerie, in true minion form, had texted Suzanne to get Sage's location. Now we were following Sage around the store, trying to get intel. But unless she forgets to scan an item at self-checkout, I wasn't sure what secrets we were supposed to uncover.

Though I noticed one thing. Valerie might be the one in enormous sunglasses, but Sage acted as if she wanted a pair too. She was hiding from people. Which didn't make sense. She should be high-fiving our old science teacher, and waving like a pageant queen on a float while she wheeled down the bread aisle.

"I think she's leaving," Valerie whispered from behind a gossip magazine she'd swiped from a passing rack. "We should get in line or we'll never get out of here in time to follow her to the next location."

"Follow her to the next location? You sound like a private investigator gone rogue. Next time, wear your fake mustache and fedora. Except there won't be a next time because this is stupid, and I'm going back to the lodge to come up with a rational plan. Alone."

Valerie curled her lip in contempt and spitefully turned the page of her magazine. "This plan has many layers. It's like an onion. Trust in the process." She dumped the magazine into the cart and winked when another register opened and everyone in front of us moved over, clearing a path in Sage's line. "Grab me a candy bar when it's your turn. All this villainy has made me hangry. Oh, and I almost forgot, your skis are ready. Don't forget to pick them up. I'll meet you back at the lodge."

Then she was gone, sliding through the crowd and disappearing into the parking lot. I met Sage's gaze across the empty gap in the line. It was too late to grab Valerie's magazine and feign interest. Instead, I wheeled the cart behind Sage and nodded a greeting, trying to appear casual.

"Who's stalking who?" Sage muttered, peering into my cart and scanning the items. Two types of cheese and a tabloid. Her eyebrow raised. "You came here just for that?"

"No." I cleared my throat, feeling heat climb my neck. "I need a chocolate bar, too. Can you pass me one from the candy rack?"

Sage hesitated as if my sugary request might be some elaborate grocery store ambush.

"Sure. Why not? I could use some chocolate therapy myself. It wasn't in the article, but I'm sure it was an oversight." She reached for the candy bar and grabbed one for herself.

"Article?"

"Never mind."

Sage passed me the candy bar, and our fingers touched. She pulled away, wiping her hand on her jacket like she had in the tea shop. My features drew together. That had to stop. She wasn't the only one still wounded from the incident in our past. We might not be friends anymore, but I was still a human being. It was hard enough being despised by everyone in town. But Sage, too?

Unacceptable.

The line moved, and Sage stacked her groceries on the conveyor belt.

Think Grayson! Say something engaging. Talking to women had always come easy because it never mattered what I said. Money talks fine on its own, and I wasn't being conceited, but I considered myself fairly attractive.

Sage acted as if I looked like a troll, and it was doing a number on my attempts at witty banter. A situation where I normally shined.

"Truffle butter, huh? Whatever happened to the kind in the plastic tubs?" I joked as Sage set an odd-looking glass jar of butter on the belt.

Her lips twitched against her will, and I was pretty sure my heart expanded inside my chest.

Not too bad for a troll.

"So, big plans for Thanksgiving?" I asked as Sage bagged her groceries. One truffle butter joke hadn't been enough to break down her walls.

"Just dinner with my parents." She swiped her card through the reader so fast it beeped angrily and she had to do it twice.

"Yeah. I have big plans too. Some friends are throwing a dinner party. Thanks for asking." Sage narrowed her eyes at me, but I kept talking, glancing at the items in my cart. "I'm gonna whip up a baked brie. Make some mozzarella Caprese."

"And do a little light reading?" Sage said, mocking my tabloid.

"Gotta keep up with those celebrity scandals. It makes for great dinner conversation."

"I bet. Good luck with your brie." Sage grabbed her groceries and made a beeline for the parking lot.

Seriously, why did every woman in my life run for the hills the second they got the chance? Was it my aftershave? I thought women loved citrus and spice. *I'm switching to pine.*

"Can you scan a little faster?" I asked the teenage clerk, who'd stopped to read the cover of my tabloid. As lame as this plan was, being around Sage was a nice distraction from my almost certain business failure.

"Face it, mister," the clerk said, scanning the magazine. "I don't think you have a shot with her."

Not unless Santa brings me a time machine for Christmas.

"What? You didn't hear my truffle butter joke? I thought I nailed that one. You try making fungi quips in the checkout line." I craned my neck, but I couldn't spot Sage through the glass windows.

The clerk shrugged and leaned toward the microphone.

"Price check on a wheel of brie." She flipped on the blinking register light. "It will just be a moment, sir."

Behind me, the line groaned, and somehow, without even trying, I climbed another notch on the villain dial.

I parked behind the antique shop and cut the engine. So far, my day had been drenched in misery. I wasn't any closer to fixing things with Sage and forget getting close enough to figure out any of her secrets.

The grocery store had nearly ended in a brawl with my price check fiasco. If I'd pulled out coupons or a checkbook, I wouldn't have made it out alive.

But that was all about to change. One of my goals with the lodge had been to restore it to its previous glory. I'd hired some help, though most of the blood, sweat, and tears of the interior remodel were my own. I salvaged as much as I could. However, I splurged on one thing.

The shop was nearly empty and closing early because of the holiday, so I made my way to the counter and hit the bell. An older gentleman with tufts of white hair, wearing wire-rimmed glasses, appeared from the back. He nodded in acknowledgment and rested his wrinkled hands on the counter.

"I should have an order ready for pickup. My assistant placed it, so it's under her name. Last name, Spellman."

"Let's see what we have." The owner ran a finger down a list of names in a ledger and tapped the page. "Yes. Here it is. I'll be right back."

I leaned against the counter, browsing a wall of vintage clocks. The sound of footsteps creaked in the back as another shopper wandered the aisles. A flash of blonde hair tucked under a familiar ski hat caught my eye, and I shook my head, positive I was seeing things.

Sage had been on my mind nonstop and now I was mistaking her for strangers.

The man returned and placed my order on the counter.

"These are perfect," I said, running my fingers over the wooden skis. The hickory had been varnished to a glossy shine and the name of the lodge was hand-painted across the front. They were going to look amazing hanging above the massive fireplace in the great room.

"They're original to the area, circa 1920, and the skis have been restored and painted by a local artisan."

The owner ran my credit card, and I signed the slip. The skis were expensive but worth the price for the added appeal of another era. While he wrapped the order, I glanced toward the back of the shop. The shopper hummed a Christmas carol, and the soft voice sounded familiar.

"Ms. Bennett, we're closing soon," the owner announced as he finished wrapping the skis.

"I'm almost finished!" Sage shouted, still hidden from view down the aisle.

No way. A surprised chuckle rumbled in my chest. What were the odds? I held up a finger, signaling to the owner I'd return to collect my skis, then quietly walked to the back of the shop.

Sage leaned close to the shelf, her hand moving in a slow circle around what appeared to be an old bowling trophy. As I watched, the words on the plaque blurred and her name appeared beneath a title.

She huffed air between her cheeks and let out a curse.

"No one is going to believe they gave me this trophy for Agent of the Year," she mumbled, removing it from the shelf to examine the faux gold statue closer. "The man is clearly bowling."

I held my breath, afraid even the whisper of air might give me away. Sage had lied about winning the award. I didn't blame her for a second. Not after witnessing the scene in her parents' tea shop and seeing the excitement around town. It was an act of preservation. I would have done the same.

But suddenly, I had leverage.

No. Walk away. You already screwed things up once.

My feet stayed rooted to the hardwood. I needed her help, and she'd made it clear she wanted nothing to do with me. If I was a better man, I'd listen. Things between us were messy enough. She'd hate me even more if I forced her to work with me.

Then again, even the Grinch had a redemption arc.

Before I changed my mind, I stepped closer, watching as she tensed.

"Caught you," I said, leaning casually against one of the shelves.

Shock morphed across her face as she recognized me, and she fumbled with the statue, accidentally letting it slip between her fingers. It hit the floor with a crash, separating the bowler's head from its body.

"Leo...it's, um, not what you think," she stammered, her cheeks going pink with embarrassment. I bit back a smile.

First, I'd found her covered in flour, and now she was adorably flustered and the perpetrator of a trophy slaying. Chaos followed her wherever she went, and it only made me want to stay close to see what would happen next.

Playing the villain had its perks, and now all I had to do was stick to the plan.

Chapter 6
Sage

I glared at Leo over the brim of my peppermint mocha. After he caught me red-handed in the antique shop, we walked across the street to get coffee so I could stall and figure out a way to explain myself. Thanks to the shop's 'You break it, you buy it' policy, my newly acquired headless bowling trophy sat next to a plate of decorated sugar cookies.

"How much did you see?" I asked.

Leo leaned back in his plush armchair and propped his ankle on his knee. Next to us, an electric heater blasted warmth over our corner of the coffee shop. It should have been cozy, romantic even, reminding me of the evenings we'd spent huddled in the lodge drinking hot chocolate long after the lifts had closed for the day. Except now, I was literally sitting in the hot seat, waiting to see if Leo knew my secret.

One of them, at least. My snow curse was still up for grabs.

"Well, let's see. You were magically altering the engraving on that trophy." He pointed to the bowler's head sitting on my napkin. "And you were mumbling about how you wouldn't fool anyone into thinking it was an agency award. So I guess I saw all of it. Are you planning to tell your parents, and by extension, the whole town, about not winning Agent of the Year?"

I inhaled a deep breath of peppermint, grimacing at the scribbled note on the cardboard that read: Congratulations, Sage! We're so proud.

My so-called achievement had made the rounds at the coffee shop. Was there no safe place? Why couldn't I have grown up off-the-grid in a bunker? My secrets would have been between me and a wall of canned peaches.

I closed my eyes to block out the glowing message and allow the festive scent to calm my irritation. Which was a lot to ask from a high-calorie attempt at aromatherapy.

"I wouldn't have to tell anyone if the shop had a wider selection of trophy options. It's difficult to alter a physical shape for more than a few seconds," I grumbled as if it were magic's fault and not my own lies. "The lettering is easier. It's more of a surface illusion. It'll last longer."

"I see. Who knew illusions were so specific?" Leo reached for his cup of coffee and took a sip. His features immediately scrunched together as if he were in pain. He set the cup back onto the table, taking a furtive glance at the older woman working behind the counter.

"Is something wrong with your coffee?" I asked, braving a sip of my own. Sweet chocolate mixed with peppermint flooded my taste buds. A dollop of whipped cream stuck to the top of my lip, and I licked it off, trying to ignore the way Leo's eyes fixated on my mouth.

Now wasn't the time to delve into *that* look. I'd been watching way too many holiday romantic comedies, and his interest was most likely all in my overactive imagination.

"The coffee is too hot." Leo hunched in his chair, and I wasn't sure I believed him. But I had bigger issues than whether he was satisfied with his beverage purchase.

"So, what do we do now? Are you going to tell my parents?" I struggled to keep the catch out of my voice. I felt like a teenager again, caught breaking the rules. This was so humiliating.

"I have a better idea." Leo plucked a cookie off my plate. "I won't tell anyone your secret if you help me out with a little project."

I scoffed. "Are you blackmailing me, Grayson? That's a dangerous game to play against a witch."

He sank his teeth into the cookie and brushed the crumbs onto the napkin. If my veiled threat bothered him, it didn't show.

"Blackmail is a harsh word, Bennett. Think of it more like a partnership. Like the one the lodge has with the tea shop."

He smiled wolfishly, hinting at his own veiled threat. Okay, so we were both brilliant at tossing up our defenses. We always had been. Him overly confident to hide any insecurity, and me, trying desperately to prove I belonged. Until, one day, those labels had fallen away, and for a blink-and-you-might-miss-it moment, I thought we were something more.

I pulled the plate of cookies out of his reach, returning his smile with one sweet enough to cause a toothache. If only it were that easy to cause someone dental pain.

I'd taken one too many strolls down memory lane today. Time to take what was left of my cookies and head home.

"What do you want from me?"

The tiniest crack in Leo's armor appeared as he shifted in the chair. He glanced again from his coffee to the woman behind the counter. Something was wrong with it. We'd been sitting here long enough for it to cool, yet he hadn't tried another sip.

My mother's words from earlier ate at the back of my mind. *They've fallen from grace.* Was it possible? Without second-guessing myself, I swiped Leo's coffee and took a sip. I'd been prepared to burn the roof of my mouth, but not for the horrid taste making my eyes water.

"Salt!" I sputtered, barely swallowing the wretched mouthful of coffee. "That's disgusting." I chased the taste with a gulp from my mocha, not caring if my entire face was covered in whipped cream.

"Give me that." Leo took his coffee and dumped the contents into the trash. When he returned, I shook my head, certain the sugar swap hadn't been an accident.

"Mrs. Avery and her husband have owned this shop for thirty years. They have the best coffee in town. Explain to me how yours tastes like drinking caffeinated seawater."

Leo let out a long sigh. "I'm surprised you haven't heard about it already. I figured they were pulling people over on the town line to let them know I was the village outcast."

"Nope, it was clear sailing. But I did see someone stuffing mailboxes with flyers. I thought it was for an estate sale, but I guess it was one of those old fashioned wanted posters. Ooh, maybe your photo is in the post office right next to mine." I let out a dry laugh, imagining our faces side-by-side in some strange plot device where instead of swapping bodies, we swapped popularity.

Leo made a face and finished the last of his cookie. "Well, let me fill you in on the town gossip. Not only have Mrs. Avery and her husband owned this shop for thirty years, but they've been married for as long. They met at the local ice skating rink, and every year on their anniversary, they returned to the rink to skate—hand in hand because apparently, some relationships can stand the test of time."

My eye twitched. I didn't care for the sarcasm in his tone or the loaded insinuation.

"So what happened?"

"My father's company bought the land and demolished the rink to build luxury condos. You know, the kind no regular person can afford."

I opened my mouth to speak, but nothing came out. Leo filled in the silence for me.

"On a related note, remember the town gazebo where the Averys had their wedding ceremony, along with just about everyone else in town? Yeah, there's a parking lot in its place now. Also, thanks to my father. Honestly, I haven't had a proper cup of coffee in this town since I arrived home. I'm surprised they let me in the door. It's only because I'm here with you."

I was stunned. I *had* missed a juicy holiday letter last year. Things with Leo were so much worse than I'd imagined. My situation seemed like a breeze. Uncontrollable snow might follow me around, but at least it wasn't an angry mob with sharpened ice skates and a mind for vengeance.

"That explains the salt," I said. As well as the dagger eyes from Mrs. Avery.

"People aren't happy I purchased the ski lodge. They're voting with their wallets and turning tourists away. Which is why I want your help." He leaned in, took a pen from his pocket, and dumped the bowler's head off the napkin, then scribbled something onto the paper.

I squinted at the handwritten agreement awaiting my signature. "You want me to help you save the ski resort, and in return, you'll help keep my secret from everyone in town?"

Leo nodded. "Until you go back to the city, no one will be the wiser. You'll leave a hero. To sweeten the deal, I even have a glass trophy you can use to pass off as your award. No physical shape-shifting required. Unless you plan to superglue that head back on and try again with the bowling trophy."

I folded my arms and studied Leo. He was serious! How had we gone from a non-starter first date, to not speaking for years, to brokering a deal on a napkin?

"You realize in my line of work, you are exactly the kind of man I would help the town get rid of. In fact, I've done it. Twice. You're the villain."

Leo's jaw tightened. "Then you'll know how to do it in reverse."

"I need time to think about it," I said, shocking myself for not turning him down flat.

"Fine. Let me know when you decide." Leo tucked the agreement into his pocket and punched his number into my phone. "I have to get back to the resort. Happy Thanksgiving, Sage," he murmured before he walked toward the exit.

Every eye in the shop watched him go. I sat there for a long moment, staring at the broken trophy.

Am I a complete fool? I should have cut him off at the knees. He tried to blackmail me! Old Sage, the woman walking around with a shattered snow globe where her heart used to be, would have thrown the bowler's head in his face.

Despite that, I'd worked enough cases to trust my instincts. By all appearances, Leo didn't deserve a second chance. But that was the funny thing about miracles. They often found you.

I pulled out my phone while I walked back to my parents' house. The first call dropped before it connected, and I had to wait until the signal bars appeared again. But my next call went through and Delia answered as I flopped backward onto my twin mattress and stared at the boy band on the ceiling.

"I need your advice," I said.

"Let me guess. You're trapped inside a guided meditation. Just follow my voice. You're getting very sleepy. Wait—that's hypnosis. What's your problem?"

I filled her in on the last few days, my newfound celebrity status, and my disastrous history with Leo.

"And the worst part is I'm considering helping the man who humiliated me and broke my heart win over the town to save his ski resort. Is that strange?"

"Yes, because you're supposed to be relaxing. Did you not get my email?"

"I did. But I'm starting to suspect self-care is a little more involved than getting fresh air and a solid eight hours of sleep." I shuddered. "I might have to heal old wounds."

Delia laughed. "No kidding. Do you think the agency initiates Operation Merry Reset because you don't use your vacation time? You have past trauma, babe."

"Why didn't you say anything?" I grumbled, punching the pillow behind my head.

"Because agent 101 is to let the subjects discover their journey organically. Remember when I told you to date, and you told me you wanted to marry your job, or something equally nasty? You can't tell someone what to do. They have to figure it out for themselves."

I blew out a breath and kicked off my boots. They hit the carpeted floor with a muffled thud. "You know, you're pretty good at this agent thing. It's only a matter of time until you get your first case."

"From your mouth to the division head's ears. So what are you going to do about your dilemma?"

"Good question. If I don't help, and the lodge goes under, my parents will lose the chance to earn extra money to replace their retirement savings. So there's plenty of guilt there. And I don't want to see the town lose another piece of its character. Even if that means helping Leo."

There was also the uncomfortable realization that I missed the person I'd been when I was with Leo and the way he made me feel. I pressed my lips into a frown. "Leo and I are adults now. I suppose I could lead with forgiveness and maturity."

Delia snorted. "That's a choice. Don't get me wrong, I'm all for maturity, but have a little fun first."

"What do you have in mind?"

"Well, Leo publicly broke your heart and made you question his sincerity. If you're planning to help the man, stuff a little payback in his Christmas stocking first. It'll make you feel good. You'll take back your power, and it might stop the snow. Then you can get your butt back here and help me get a date with Simon."

I shook my head. Delia was persistent, I'd give her that. "I'm hanging up, now."

"Okay! Good luck with healing your wounds. Bring me back a souvenir. Something expensive. Bye!"

Take back my power, huh? If there was one thing absent in my life, it was a certain level of joy. And joy seemed like a mandatory quality for someone responsible for doling out miracles. Somewhere along the line, I'd become so consumed with proving myself, I'd forgotten to have any fun.

Revenge might be exactly what the doctor ordered.

I grabbed a notebook on the bedside table and opened it to a blank page. If the town wanted an agent of the year, they'd get her.

Chapter 7
Leo

The microwave beeped, and I carried my turkey dinner to the lobby, dropping the plastic dish onto the reservation counter. Gravy puddled around the mashed potatoes and steam rose from the small scoop of stuffing. It looked edible, but far from the home-cooked meal I longed for. Then again, I had to make do with what was in the freezer aisle.

We only had a couple of rooms booked and we closed the lifts early, so I sent the staff home for the holiday, planning to man the hotel myself. No one questioned the strange, last-minute cancellation of my dinner plans. Because they knew the truth. My big, fancy Thanksgiving dinner was about as real as my mashed potatoes.

There was no baked brie and no mozzarella Caprese. No one wanted to share a meal with the man who ruined the town.

My father was overseas with his mistress, and my mother had checked herself into a spa for an extended stay of exfoliation and seaweed wraps, as she did for most holidays. That left me to the microwaveable feast cooling on the counter.

I checked my phone and loaded my fork with a chunk of rubbery turkey. Sage hadn't responded to my offer. I'd decided to call it that because the term blackmail bothered me.

What didn't bother me these days? It was hard to stay positive in the face of so much negativity. I never expected to return home, hoping for a clean slate, only to spend the holidays alone in my empty ski lodge.

Been there, already bought the T-shirt.

Maybe this was a mistake. Both coming home and buying this frozen dinner. *Rock bottom—it turns out—is just a lake of gelatinous turkey gravy.*

"Hello? Is anyone there?"

I paused, the fork suspended in the air as Sage's voice echoed through the lobby. She dusted fresh snow from her jacket and peered at the vaulted ceilings. Then she did a slow circle, admiring the polished hardwood floors, oversized sofas in front of the hearth, and finally the giant stone fireplace. Her gaze remained fixed on the vintage skis I'd mounted over the mantel.

A smile touched her lips.

It faded slightly, taking a bit of my hope with it when she spotted me standing behind the reservation counter.

"Oh. I thought you'd be out to dinner. I tried texting, but the service in this town stinks. If I was staying, I'd switch providers. Maybe get a satellite phone. I hear they work well in the mountains." She cleared her throat; cheeks flushing their telltale pinkish hue. Removing her mittens, she reached into the canvas tote bag slung over her shoulder and removed a folded piece of paper. "Sorry. I'm rambling. I was going to leave you a note."

Notes were bad news. No one wanted a note. I hadn't expected her to turn me down, and now I faced the realization I never had any leverage because I had no intention of revealing her secret. Some blackmailer I turned out to be.

She stepped up to the counter but didn't hand over the paper. Instead, she furrowed her brow and stared at my dinner. Nope—*This* was officially rock bottom. Beneath the lake of gelatinous gravy was a sandy bed of shame where people you care about discover you're eating Thanksgiving dinner alone.

"It's not what it looks like," I quipped, tossing back the same phrase she'd said when I caught her in the antique shop.

"It never is, is it?" Her hand dipped into the canvas bag a second time and she pulled out a large plastic container. Setting it on the counter, she removed the lid. "I felt bad for whoever was stuck working the reservation desk, so I grabbed some leftovers. My dad makes a mean turkey, and my mom handles the sweet potatoes."

"What did you make?" I asked, my voice unusually hoarse.

She pointed to the thick dollop of jellied berries. "The cranberry sauce. I promise it's not from a can."

She could have popped it out of a can and sliced it into cubes, and it was still going to be the best thing I'd ever eaten. But homemade? There were no words.

"Here, I'll save you a trip to the microwave."

She walked over to the hearth and held her hands in front of the flames. The warm glow of the fire flickered over her slender frame and made her blonde hair gleam. Years had passed, and I found I was still as drawn to her as I'd always been. It wasn't difficult to imagine our lives turning out another way. But this wasn't one of those sappy holiday movies where a glimpse into an alternate future was enough to fix the past.

After a minute, she returned and placed her palms around the plastic container until steam rose from the inside. "It's the witchy version of heat conduction. Careful, it's hot."

I speared a piece of turkey and slid it through the cranberry sauce. My eyes widened at the first bite, and I had to control a groan of pleasure. How could such a simple combination of food taste like a feeling?

Slow down...savor it.

"I remember your warming trick. Your toes were freezing, and you warmed your boots after each ski lesson. I wouldn't let you touch mine."

"Because you thought I was going to melt the bindings!"

I shrugged. "They were expensive."

The room settled into a restless quiet while I ate the leftovers. Our memories were a minefield. Watch your step or one might explode in your face.

Sage wandered the lobby, examining the finer details of my attempt at renovation, while I watched her, wondering when she was going to reveal her hand.

I wanted to know what she thought of the place. If she would have done anything different. Had I done the lodge justice? And most of all, would she believe me if I told her I hated the way things ended between us?

But I stayed quiet and savored the sweet potatoes, afraid if I asked the wrong question, she might leave.

The last bite came too quickly, like most good things, ending far before you were ready. Sage approached the counter.

"I don't suppose you have any pie in that magic bag of yours?" I asked, half-joking, half the most serious I'd ever been in my life.

She rolled her eyes, and I nearly fell over when she removed a second container with a single slice of pumpkin pie.

"You're greedy, you know that?"

"Comes with being a small-town degenerate. I can't help myself."

Flattening her lips into a thin line, she collected the empty container and put it back inside her bag. A few bites of pie and this whole charade would be over. I was almost afraid to finish it.

But then she surprised me.

"I decided I'm in. I accept your obvious attempt at blackmail."

"Offer," I clarified, determined to keep that unsavory word off the table.

"Is that what we're calling it?"

I nodded, challenging her over a forkful of pie.

"Fine. Then I accept your *offer*."

I couldn't believe the plan had worked. For the first time since I'd arrived home, I might have a chance to turn things around.

"Great!" I said, disbelief lingering in my tone. "Welcome to Team Villain. We wear black on Wednesdays and chisel candy canes into shivs."

Sage shook her head, trying her best to keep a straight face. "Nice. I love arts and crafts. What days do we sing toxic Christmas carols and burn gingerbread cookies?"

I grinned, not bothering to hide my satisfaction, and slid over the empty pie dish. "I'll check the calendar."

Another awkward silence stretched between us as if we didn't know whether we should slip back into our old ways or keep our distance. Sage shuffled her feet and opened her mouth to speak, but closed it again with a nervous breath.

"Do you...want a cup of coffee?" I asked, gesturing to the coffee station I'd refreshed on the off chance a guest stopped in the lobby. "Salt-free. I swear. Though I have a heavy hand with the grinds, so it might be a little strong."

"Um. Yeah, okay." She hesitated for a second, then dove into action, preparing two steaming cups. "I should let you know what you're in for. I put together a plan to help save the lodge, but I'll need your approval."

"What's your idea?" I took one of the coffee cups and rounded the reservation desk to claim a spot on the sofa. Sage sat at the other end of the couch, crossing her legs beneath her. There was an empty span of upholstery between us, but it was a start.

"I went over all the options. Since Team Villain can't use a nefarious device to brainwash everyone, the only way to heal your rift with the town this season is to fix the past. You've spent all of your energy restoring the lodge. Now we have to restore their faith." Sage pulled out her phone and opened a file, then zoomed in. "I reviewed the resort's property survey online, and right here—" She tapped the screen. "Is the perfect place to rebuild the skating rink and the gazebo. What do you think?"

Excitement gleamed in her eyes, but my stomach dropped. It was the perfect plan. Restoring the rink and building the gazebo would bring in more tourists and families to the resort. The gazebo specifically would be great for outdoor events and private parties. Both features would increase revenue while bringing back a memorable pastime. The downside was it cost money I didn't have.

"Are you sure you don't know any coercion spells? Because I can't afford to rebuild the rink. I can handle the gazebo if nobody minds a DIY project. But there isn't a budget for anything else."

Sage's features softened. "I had a feeling finances might be an issue. My parents mentioned you've been doing most of the work yourself. Honestly, the place looks great. Remember, there used to be holes in the wall over there?" Sage pointed to where I'd arranged small tables for guests to have drinks in front of the windows. "And it was so drafty! The carpet always smelled like wet feet, and someone had the bright idea to use plaid wallpaper by the reservation desk."

"Yeah, the wallpaper was awful, and the radiator never worked right. If you didn't sit close enough to the fireplace to test the flammability statement on your jacket, you'd freeze."

Sage nodded and sipped her coffee. "Which is why I always had to warm my boots." Her gaze returned to the mantel where I'd hung the skis. "I remember those, too. They look like the pair your great-grandfather had."

"I can't believe you recognize them."

"Well, you dragged me through a lesson on the history of skiing with an extensive portion of show and tell. It was *so boring*, but also kind of endearing. You're a bit of a ski nerd."

"There is no such thing!"

She scooted closer, closing the expansive upholstery gap. "There is too." Our eyes held for a long moment before the teasing glint slipped from her gaze. She looked away and self-consciously rubbed the back of her neck. "Um. Anyways. Back to the point. Even if you had the money to burn and wanted to build both attractions on your own, it's not the way. You want the town to feel like they're involved. Bringing the community together for this project is as important as where it's located. Which is why I'm proposing a series of fundraisers."

A rough laugh escaped my throat. "They'd throw cupcakes in my face if I tried to host a bake sale."

"Oh, you will not be baking. I saw your attempt at a turkey dinner. Leave the fundraising to me. All you have to do is show up." She leaned in, resting her elbows on her knees. Her blonde hair brushed softly against her shoulders, and the fire warmed the splash of freckles across her cheeks. "Trust me, Leo."

My fingers pressed into my palm before I did the unthinkable and defied the remaining space between us.

"I trust you," I said, not sure if I trusted myself.

Sage exhaled a heavy breath, her nervous smile returning. She leaned back, breaking the spell, and checked the time on her phone. The room felt colder; ice flowing into the crack that had fractured our connection.

"I have to go. I slipped away while my parents were in a turkey coma." She reached into her pocket to remove the note she'd written for me and tapped the folder paper. "Inside are directions. Meet me at that location first thing on Saturday morning. No excuses. No complaints. You asked for my help. Remember that."

I lifted my hands, palms out, in defense. "You're the professional. I'll concede to your wisdom."

She finished her coffee and handed me the empty cup. "Bring my trophy with you, and you better keep your end of the bargain. We made a deal."

"Consider it done."

Sage grabbed her bag and put on her mittens before heading toward the door. "Oh, and one other thing. Have your assistant send me your clothing measurements."

"Why?" I asked, suspicion thick in my voice. "Are you planning to knit me one of those ugly Christmas sweaters? Is that our new team uniform?"

Sage flashed me a smile that was mostly teeth. "You'll have to wait and see, partner. Happy Thanksgiving!"

Chapter 8
Sage

"This is somehow the most perfect and the most appalling thing I've ever seen." I unhooked the elf costume from the rack and laid it flat on the dressing room table.

Leo's assistant, Valerie, peered over my shoulder and let out a snort that was anything but delicate. "It's the green velvet tunic that does it for me."

"Really? I love the faux fur around the cuffs and the red and white striped knee socks. They're so whimsical. You're sure this will fit?" I asked, jingling the bell sewn into the tip of the felt hat.

"I'm positive. I sneaked into Leo's closet and took detailed measurements."

Valerie was nothing, if not precise. I liked her immediately when we met for drinks to discuss my plan and arrange Leo's schedule. She'd been sworn to secrecy about the first step in my strategy to save the resort, and seeing as how Leo hadn't strapped on a pair of skis and raced out of town, I knew I'd found a trustworthy ally.

"It's almost time. Where's our soon-to-be reluctant elf?" I peeked outside the dressing room, already hearing the commotion from the families standing in line outside our Santa's pop-up village.

The visit with Santa was an annual event in town with a line that usually snaked around the street. This year was no different. We'd had to bribe one of the volunteers to take the day off, but Valerie had worked her magic and offered him a free lift ticket. Hit the slopes or spend the day trying to entertain children tired of waiting in line? To him, it was a no-brainer. To us, it was the spot we needed to put the plan in motion.

"Leo's on his way. I may have hinted this was going to be part of an advertising campaign and there would be cameras."

"There will be cameras all right. But I don't think he's going to want to be in front of one."

Valerie pressed a fist against her mouth to keep from laughing, then grabbed a mini candy cane from the basket of favors. "I'll go wait in the parking lot and make sure he comes in through the back so it won't ruin the surprise."

"Try to grab his keys so he won't have access to a getaway car."

"Ooh, good call."

The mischievous gleam in her eyes was catchy, but I couldn't help the nerves whipping around like snow flurries inside my stomach. I took a long, deep breath as Valerie slipped out of the dressing room and shut the door. I'd never been this unsettled handling a case before. Then again, a case had never felt so personal, or so emotionally precarious.

Running into Leo again hadn't gone the way I'd expected. I thought if it ever happened, I'd do one of those epic power moves where I strut past, hair blowing in the wind, while he watched in agony, realizing his great loss.

Instead, after the tea shop incident and a grocery store run-in, I ended up feeding him my homemade cranberry sauce. Then I forked over the last piece of pie, all while dressed in my Thanksgiving sweatpants.

I'd put a moratorium on memory lane, then threw the gates open myself, the moment I spotted an old pair of skis. I might as well have shouted from the mountaintop that I remember everything about our time together. Every story. Every joke. All the way to the bitter end.

The only agony in our reunion was mine, and I should be hiding under a blanket with a punchbowl of spiked eggnog, but weirdly, I wouldn't have changed anything.

I think my heart broke a little seeing him eating that awful frozen meal alone. Especially on a day reserved for spending time with family and friends. It reminded me of eating alone in the school cafeteria, watching everyone around me laugh and trade their snacks. I always wished I could be anyone else. Even if it was just until the bell rang.

Maybe it was the maturity—I glanced again at the elf costume—okay, definitely not the maturity. But there was something to be said about examining your past and giving someone a second chance. If I had done my glorious power move, I wouldn't have recognized myself in Leo, or witnessed his hard work in restoring the lodge.

I certainly wouldn't have cozied up to him on the sofa and waited anxiously to hear his thoughts on my plan, or felt a flutter of warmth when he put his trust in me. *I blame the rustic charm and heat from the fireplace, and that's the mantle I'm dying on.*

Leo had once helped me feel less alone, and while it hadn't mattered as much to him as it did to me, now our roles were reversed. We might only be working together because of our bargain, but helping people around Christmastime was my calling, and award or no award, I was absurdly good at it.

There was a knock at the door, and Leo entered wearing a dark pair of sunglasses. His hair had an effortless windswept look, and he wore one of those cable-knit sweaters with the zipper pulled down a few inches. The glasses came off with one smooth motion, and he slanted me an irresistible smile.

"I'm ready for my close-up." Leo cocked his head, allowing a lock of hair to fall flawlessly in front of his eye. "You probably don't know this about me, but I have done some modeling in the past."

My lips trembled. Delia was right. Revenge was the sweetest thing on earth. *Never skimp on the revenge.*

I bit my cheek hard before I gave myself away. "I thought you had. Your previous experience is going to help you shine today."

"So what am I wearing? Is it a laid-back leather jacket in front of a roaring fireplace? Will there be an adoring golden retriever and a green screen?"

Valerie was my hero. She couldn't have prepped him better.

"No dog, I'm afraid, but there will be plenty of green." I picked up the elf costume in one hand, then grabbed the black ankle boots with curled toes in the other.

Leo's features froze in horror. "I'm not wearing that."

"You are, and you better hurry. The kids are getting anxious." I shook the costume and gestured with the boots toward the changing screen.

The glee fell from my lips as Leo's eyes darkened; the brown molasses of his iris' turning to coal.

He stepped closer, his shoulders bunching beneath the cable-knit sweater. Each thud of his boots echoed in my ears, warning me to toss the costume and make a run for it.

Thud... This was a mistake!

Thud... He was joking about the candy cane shivs, right?

Thud... Honestly? Leo in villain mode was kind of hot.

I held my ground. Forget burnout. I needed a top ten list of ways to stop lusting after the man who wanted to wring my neck.

Cue mindful breathing...or any breathing at all.

My heart tripped over itself as his mouth dropped to my ear. A sizzling moment passed where neither of us moved. His fingers closed over mine, taking the hanger from my hand at the same time his warm breath brushed my cheek.

"Well played, Bennett. I hope you're keeping score."

I exhaled a shuddery breath when he moved past me and disappeared behind the dressing screen. *Sweet snowballs that was intense.* Revenge might be exquisite, but it had a mean sucker-punch. It also strangely smelled like pine. Had Leo changed his aftershave?

"You forgot the shoes," I mumbled, still dazed enough to step behind the screen.

Leo had removed his sweater, and I got an eyeful of toned shoulders, corded arms, and abs that had no right hiding beneath wool—or any type of fiber for that matter. Fool that I was, I stared. For way longer than I should.

Worth it. Do what brings you joy.

Of course, he caught me. *You tend to notice when you're half-naked and someone is standing next to you holding a ridiculous pair of elf shoes.*

He took the shoes—completely shameless—a knowing gleam radiating in his eyes. "Thanks. I think there's a hat, too."

"Right, the hat." I stumbled away from the screen, pressing my fingers into the bridge of my nose. What was wrong with me? I acted like I'd never seen a man's chest before or hadn't been the driving force in creating last year's Flame and Frost calendar. Twelve months of seasonal wonders, all in the name of raising money for a local fire station. Talk about a fundraiser. I still had mine hanging by the closet.

"You're supposed to be a professional," I grumbled under my breath. "Stop imagining Leo as Mr. December and act like one."

Valerie knocked and poked her head through the door. "How is everything going in here?"

I grabbed the hat and glanced over at the dressing screen. "We're both still alive, though barely. He'll be ready in a minute."

Valerie crooked her finger and coaxed me closer. "We have a problem."

"What's the matter? Are people leaving?"

"No, nothing like that. The other elf never showed, and well, Santa needs two." She slipped another hanger holding a costume through the gap in the door.

Alarm slithered up my spine. "No, he doesn't. You're making that up."

"Sorry. It's in his contract. I would fill in. I really would. But I have to prepare for the thing we talked about." Her eyebrows wriggled with conspiratorial delight. "So you're up. Both of you are on in five," she said, shutting the door in my face.

"No, wait!" I whisper-shouted, now holding the smaller, female version of Leo's elf costume.

This wasn't how it was supposed to go. I was meant to look cute and polished while Leo was set to look like he'd just stepped off the red eye from the North Pole.

I looked daggers at the green dress with red trim and cinched leather belt. The gold buckle twinkled in the overhead light, mocking me.

"Was that Valerie? That woman took my car keys and now I know why." Leo had finished changing and stood behind me, rifling through the basket of mini candy canes. "Are these for us too?" he asked, popping one out of the plastic wrapper and sticking it under his tongue. His gaze bounced between my panic-stricken expression and the elf costume in my hand.

It wasn't difficult to infer what had happened.

He sucked on the candy cane. "I know you tried to embarrass me, Bennett. But you can't. Because I look good. Even in this getup. Seems like your plan failed, and now you have to wear one, too."

"My plans do not fail." I swept past him toward the changing screen. "No peeking!" I shouted over the top of the wall.

Leo chuckled. "I would never. That's your job."

I clenched my jaw and shimmied out of my skinny jeans. Maybe the costume wouldn't fit. What were the odds that the girl who didn't show was my exact size? Then again, what were the odds Leo could pull off an elf costume? He looked goofy, of course, but in a sexy way, like he was in on the joke and confident enough to pull it off.

"Revenge only works in the movies," I muttered as I buttoned the front of the velvet A-line dress. The skirt fell above my knees and the belt fit snugly around my waist. I slipped my striped stockinged feet into the pointed shoes and sighed.

This was happening. Might as well make the best of it. I'd save a reindeer. It was only a matter of time before I played Santa's helper, too.

I stepped from behind the screen and planted my hands on my hips. "Don't say a word."

The candy cane crunched between Leo's teeth. He went still; his gaze dipping to my boots, sliding slowly up my stockings, then settled somewhere around my fur neckline.

"Stop it!" I hissed. "This is a family event. That is not a PG-rated look."

I should know, I gave the same look a trial run not ten minutes ago.

"You started it." He leaned in, settling the elf hat on my head with a soft jingle. "So what's the plan, boss?"

The plan? Right—the plan that did not include dragging Leo behind the dressing screen so I could manifest a little more of my missing joy.

I squared my shoulders. "The plan is to hand out candy canes. Smile at folks, and when I announce your proposal to rebuild the skating rink and gazebo at the resort, do exactly as I say."

"Great. You're going to start a riot at a kid's event. Have you thought through scarring children's memories of the time they met Santa? Instead of an elf, I should dress up as Freddy Kreuger."

I placed both hands on Leo's shoulders and forcefully turned him toward the door. He grabbed the basket of candy canes before I pushed him through.

"It's showtime," I said as we walked side-by-side into Santa's village like two elves going into a tinsel-strewn battle.

Chapter 9
Sage

"I thought you preferred toxic caroling," Leo said, angling his head toward the group of festive singers decked out in red and green, greeting families as they approached Santa's insulated tent. Multi-colored lights and giant bows decorated the space, while velvet ropes with gold stanchions contained the kids line, eager for their turn.

I took in the delicious scent of cinnamon mixed with the faint aroma of cocoa and elbowed Leo in the ribs.

"Just smile. You're doing great."

"I am smiling. I think my face might be frozen in this position. I may never frown again. What's a villain to do?"

I jabbed him again and nodded innocently as a mother chased her daughter to a stop in front of Leo's basket full of candy canes. He offered the kid one, then winked and pulled another one from behind her ear. The girl giggled and clutched both candy canes to her heart before racing off into Santa's tent.

"You do magic, too?" I groaned. This plan was a disaster! Yes—it was brilliant and already starting to work—but it was impossible to stay mad at a handsome elf who could do party tricks. Where was my shrewd internal voice to warn me of the consequences of my actions? Was she also drunk on Leo's appeal, like some tipsy sprite who fell into the holiday punch-bowl?

"Don't be jealous. You're still the best witch in town."

Pressing a hand to the small of my back, he moved me closer to the portable heater and held out the basket as another family passed.

Ugh, chivalry is alive and well and looks good in a felt hat.

I needed to focus. While it had been fun seeing everyone's surprised reaction to Leo's participation, there were plenty of disapproving looks in the crowd. Thankfully, there were a few appreciative ones as well. Many from frazzled parents, happy for a quick breather while Leo amused a child waiting to see Santa with a joke.

The amount of dad jokes he had up his sleeve was both alarming and weirdly attractive.

"So, when does the riot start?" Leo asked, eyeing the line that had dwindled.

We'd been Santa's sentries for a couple of hours, and though the meet and greet portion of the day was almost over, many who'd come through the line still mingled in the square waiting for the announcement I'd teased in Friday's edition of the Gazette.

The carolers kept the crowd entertained and food vendors supplied them with sweet treats and warm drinks. I checked my phone, confirming Valerie was ready for part two of the plan.

"I think now's a good time. Leave the basket," I said, grabbing Leo's sleeve and tugging him through the crowd. We made our way toward a raised platform setup with a microphone stand. Off to the side was a giant red curtain, with Valerie manning a rope mechanism.

This was where things got tricky, and the whole plan could go off the rails. If Leo balked or no one agreed to play, the day would slide right into awkward territory. Leo's riot could become a reality.

But I'd learned two things since coming home. First, Leo was surprisingly game for anything, and second, sometimes it was healthy—and a lot of fun—to let people vent their frustrations in a constructive way.

If this worked, the town might finally see Leo as more than his father's shadow, and not someone willing to strip away what made this town special.

This moment mattered.

The town needed to remember Leo was one of them. That he could dive into their traditions with enthusiasm. They needed to see his vulnerability and willingness to face their anger head-on, even if that anger was misplaced. After all, steam only dissipated if given the opportunity.

If they could laugh together, it might be enough to break through their icy barrier. Or I might just be a witch, dressed in an elf costume, spouting tea shop wisdom, and hoping for a miracle.

I stepped up to the microphone and waited for the crowd to go quiet. I cleared my throat, hoping my nerves would settle once I got started. Since becoming an agent, I'd spoken at plenty of events, yet this felt like a new challenge.

My confidence wavered as I sized up the familiar faces. Every instinct urged me to hide the person I used to be, but I was asking Leo to put himself out there. Maybe I needed to do the same thing, too.

"Hello everyone, and welcome to today's event. My name is Sage Bennett, and for those who don't know me, I grew up here. I'm the reason no one is allowed to eat or drink anything at the high school science fair."

The crowd chuckled, warming to my speech. I smoothed my anxious hands down my waist and kept going.

"But sleep potions aside, I know you're all waiting for the big announcement, and I won't keep you in suspense any longer. We all know Leo Grayson is the new owner of the ski lodge, and it's no secret there's some unfavorable history there. I tried to attack him with a whisk in the tea shop when I first arrived home, and that was before I even knew about the lodge. Sorry about all the flour, Dad," I said, waving when I spotted him in the crowd unwrapping a slab of fried dough dusted with powdered sugar. He gave me a thumbs up, then went back to eating his snack while my mother leaned in and most likely scolded him about his sugar intake.

"That said, I'm here to tell you Leo wants to make things right. He knows what you've lost and he plans to rebuild the community skating rink and a new gazebo on the resort grounds."

A murmur of surprise flowed through the crowd.

"Let me tell you why this matters. Tradition is important in this town. The memories we have skating each winter, or sharing some of the most cherished moments of our lives under the gazebo, shouldn't go away because of a business deal. Our voices matter. Our landmarks matter.

"But the thing is, Leo can't do it alone. That's where you come in. We've planned a series of fundraisers to help get this project off the ground in the hopes we can fund the rink by Christmas. The first fundraiser starts right now, and Leo has volunteered to take the plunge!" I pointed to Valerie waiting on the sidelines. She nodded and tugged on the rope, pulling the curtain back to reveal a giant dunk tank filled with a ball pit that resembled a mountain of snowballs.

I glanced at Leo to get his reaction. He'd dropped his head into his hands, but there was a smile toying with his lips, and he hadn't bolted, so I pressed onward.

"That's right—today you get to dunk Leo—our fearless elf. For charity, of course. Each shot helps fund the rink, and it's a great way to let off a little steam. I know I have some aggravation to get out. This elf gear is itchy." I picked up a softball and tossed it in the air, catching it in my palm. "So, who's up first?"

I searched the crowd, hoping desperately for a volunteer.

No one moved. The gathering had gone eerily silent. A cough echoed in the air, and you could hear the crinkling of the wrapper from my dad's fried dough.

Disappointment tangled around the growing icicle in my chest. Worse than subjecting Leo to this public display was seeing him twist in the wind. His open-minded smile had vanished, and I felt it like a punch to the gut. I knew at that moment how much their acceptance meant to him.

The same way I had longed to feel accepted. This wasn't some silly bargain where I helped him recoup his investment. This was his life.

"I'll give it a shot." The voice broke through the silence in the crowd.

Mrs. Avery, the owner of the coffee shop, stepped forward, approaching the raised platform. Relief melted through me, but I braved a glance at Leo. Mrs. Avery had poured salt in his drink, and now she was going to pour salt in his wounds. This was the best possible outcome or a potential death knell in my plan. *Tough to call.*

Leo straightened his shoulders, giving me a look that spoke volumes. He still trusted me. *Please, please, please, don't let this plan fail,* I chanted as he took his place inside the tank.

Mrs. Avery handed over a crisp five-dollar bill, and I handed her the softball. The crowd watched with a tense stillness as she stood on the marked spot and stared at her opponent.

I wasn't sure if I was going to throw up or sing "*Joy to the World*".

Mrs. Avery drew back her arm and let the ball fly.

It was off the mark, slightly higher than it should have been. With a flick of my wrist, I sent a gust of air to weigh it down. A second later, it slammed into the target.

Leo's eyes widened as the seat beneath him released, dropping him into the ball pit. He swam through plastic to the surface, his elf hat lost somewhere in the pit. When his eyes found mine again, I knew he saw me rig it. He mouthed the words 'well played' and flashed me a two and, then a zero with his fingers.

Mrs. Avery had tears in her eyes. She laughed and wiped at her lashes.

"That felt surprisingly good," she said, then faced the crowd. "I say we give this boy a chance. Let him prove us wrong. Because I'd love nothing more than to lace up my skates again! Who's next?"

Hands shot in the air as a line formed. The carolers broke into another song while Valerie swooped in to collect donations.

I stepped outside of the crush, watching from the sidelines as excitement swelled. Dropping my head back, I studied the cloudless sky. It hadn't snowed once since I'd agreed to help Leo. That might be a coincidence, but it might also be progress. I certainly felt more like myself than I had in a long time.

"Hot chocolate for my clever girl?" my dad asked, joining me with a cup topped with mini marshmallows.

"Yes, please!" I accepted the cup and sucked a few of the marshmallows into my mouth.

"It's good to see you two kids' friends again." My dad kept his gaze on the dunk tank as Leo took another plunge.

"I wouldn't go that far," I said, cringing at the frost in my tone. "I'm helping him out with this project. Nothing more than that. Besides, we were never that close." I rubbed my arms, trying to ward off the chill. "It's complicated."

He sighed and clapped a hand on my shoulder. "Never seemed that complicated to me. We miss having you home, you know. It seems like you ran off there for a little while."

"I needed a reset," I said, amused by the comparison between Old Sage and the agency's initiative for sending me home.

"Try to have some fun while you're here. Don't work too hard."

"Doesn't it look like I'm having fun?" I asked, tilting my head until the bell on my elf hat jingled.

He chuckled and squeezed my shoulder. "That was a good speech. You should be proud of yourself—forget what everyone else thinks. Including your mother. She means well."

"Thanks, Dad."

"Finish your hot chocolate. I'll go relieve that boy. I'm sure Leo's ready for a break, and I've always wanted to sit in one of those things. Plus, your mother will empty her wallet to see me drop."

The sun had set, and the twinkling lights shined brighter as I walked through the square, stopping to chat or joke about who had the best throwing arm. The frosty air puffed in white clouds in front of my face, and I could barely feel my toes in the poorly insulated boots.

Elves might live in the North Pole, but their clothes weren't made for the cold weather.

"There you are." Leo pushed his way through a group of people listening to a local band that had replaced the carolers. "Geez, you look freezing." He reached for my hands, sandwiching them between his own, then blew hot air against our skin. "Do you have any idea how much money we've raised from the dunk tank alone? And Valerie said others have promised to stop by the lodge and contribute. There are still a few naysayers, but people are coming around. You are incredible."

I blushed, trying not to enjoy Leo's touch too much. I was cold enough that if he gave me the opening, I'd launch myself at him to see if my witchy heat conduction thing worked on body heat.

"Santa's the real hero. I just work for him."

Leo chuckled. "Such a modest witch."

"You did good today. I thought for sure you were going to run when Valerie pulled back the curtain."

"I thought about it. But have you tried to run in these shoes? What's more embarrassing: a dunk tank or slip-sliding away in an elf costume?"

"Good point."

"Hey, Mr. Grayson, over here!" A man with a camera and a lanyard waved to get Leo's attention. The man jogged over as I pulled my hands from Leo's and folded them against my chest to maintain the warmth.

"Can I get your picture for the paper? We're going to run an article on the rink construction and it would be great if you could answer some questions."

"Sure," Leo said.

I stepped out of the frame, letting him have his moment, but Leo reached for me again and pulled me against his side. He wrapped his arm around my waist, and I looked up in shock as the camera snapped a photo.

"Smile for the paper," he murmured.

Another snap of the camera forced my gaze away, even as Leo drew me closer, tucking the top of my head under his chin.

"I'm glad you're back, Bennett," he said, lowering his voice so only I could hear.

My throat tightened as if it could stop my response, but I forced the words out, anyway. "I'm not staying."

His long exhale ruffled my hair. "Then I guess you're mine until Christmas."

Chapter 10

Sage

You're mine until Christmas.

The words echoed in my mind as I stared at my phone, examining the photo of Leo and I that ran in last week's paper. One thing was certain: my emotions were more tangled than a ball of Christmas lights left in the attic for too long.

Leo was doing it on purpose. He was twisting me up and making me confuse our bargain with something more. Maybe he thought it was funny or a way to pass the time until a better prospect came along.

Winning over the town means the villain transforms into Cold Spell's most eligible bachelor.

It was practically the premise for a hit reality show. Except I wasn't the girl who got the rose, but one of the behind-the-scenes producers who never had a shot in the first place.

Hadn't I learned my lesson the first time? I couldn't let history repeat itself, and I would not fall head over heels again for someone who wasn't serious.

I checked the calendar. There were only three weeks left until Christmas, and I was due in Wood Pine for my next case in a few days. Which meant I needed to secure the money for the rink, make sure my snowfall companion had hit the road for good, and then get out of town as soon as possible.

We'd made a nice dent with our first fundraiser and spent the last week collecting items from local businesses for an upcoming raffle at the lodge. We planned the event to boost attendance for my parents' afternoon tea reception and planned to offer a wide selection of finger foods alongside a few craft cocktails for people looking for something a little spicier than tea.

Preparing the menu for a large crowd had made my dad the happiest I'd ever seen him, and I felt confident the tea shop was in a good place after learning about its previous rough patch. Now that things were rolling, my presence at the next fundraiser wasn't required. Valerie was perfectly capable of working from my notes to finish organizing things.

Besides, there was still the not-insignificant problem of my fake award. Leo had given me one of his skiing trophies after the Santa event. It would make the perfect decoy, composed of a faceted crystal with an engraving which would be simple to alter. But I hadn't mustered the courage to do it. The crystal ruse was currently stuffed under a pile of extra blankets in my bedroom closet.

With all the excitement around the skating rink, my achievement was yesterday's news. Let's hope it stayed that way for a couple more days until I made my escape.

I glanced again at the photo, then against my better judgment, I quickly saved it to my camera roll and flipped the device over so I wouldn't be tempted to stare at it some more.

Leo, dressed in an elf costume with his arms wrapped around me, was not this year's Christmas card—or any other year, for that matter! It belonged in the depths of my camera roll, buried under a mountain of cute cat photos.

Grabbing my notebook with the rest of my ideas, I went downstairs and found my parents eating breakfast.

"Want me to make you an egg?" Dad asked me as I filled a thermos with hot coffee.

"No. Toast is fine." I snagged a piece slathered in jelly from the plate on the counter and stuffed it into my mouth.

"You're too skinny. Have an egg," Mom said, studying me over the edge of her newspaper. "Betsy's granddaughter is a nutritionist. She says it's important to start your day with protein."

"I like to start my day with a donut." Dad winked.

Mom folded the newspaper and set it next to her plate. "Don't encourage her, David."

I counted to three, then forced a patient smile. "I don't have time for encouragement or an egg. I'm heading to the lodge to drop off my notebook to Valerie. I'm going to let her take over the next event. She'll do a great job."

Mom sipped her tea, then placed the cup gently back into the saucer. "Leo's assistant is very attractive. I wouldn't be surprised if something was going on between those two."

"Suzanne," Dad warned.

"What? It's only a matter of time. Everyone's talking about it. Leo hasn't dated a single woman since he returned home. True—he has been the town pariah, but that's not the case anymore. And a man with his looks doesn't stay on the market long. Imagine. The next wedding we have under the gazebo could be a Grayson wedding!"

I choked down the last bite of toast and chased it with a gulp from my thermos. The coffee tasted sour in my mouth. Leo wasn't interested in Valerie. Was he? My mom lived to gossip, and that's all it was.

Gossip that made my stomach burn.

"I have to go," I said, slipping on my jacket and grabbing my bag.

The front door closed with more force than I intended, rattling in the frame. I scowled at the sky, noting the gray clouds gathering over the house.

"Don't you dare snow," I threatened.

A single snowflake drifted lazily from above and landed squarely on my nose.

I closed my eyes and took a few deep breaths. Leo's potential wedding under a newly minted gazebo didn't matter when I was getting the heck out of Cold Spell. I'd finish my last case for the year, and then I'd take a real vacation.

To a beach on an actual tropical island.

With white sand and gorgeous men who deliver you drinks in a coconut.

Yeah—I was going to Fiji. Eat your heart out, Grayson.

When I forced my eyes back open, the storm clouds were gone, and I felt centered and ready to check flight schedules.

But first, the notebook. I requested a ride to the resort and got out in front of the lodge.

In the time since we'd announced the rink project, there'd already been an increase in visitors to the resort. Skiers sailed past on their way to the lift, and guests with luggage stacked at their feet waited to check into the hotel.

A bit of pride expanded inside my chest. I was good at my job. The proof was right in front of me. While this trip was mostly a lesson in futility mixed with a confusing Ghost of Christmas Past reenactment, there was one merit: sweet validation.

I climbed the steps to the lodge, bypassing the line at the reservation desk, and spotted Valerie with a giant marker, coloring in the bottom of a cardboard cutout thermometer. It was already halfway full.

"Hey, Sage!" She dusted her hands on her black dress pants and waved me over. "I updated our goal marker. What do you think?"

I eyed her critically, noticing her flawless complexion when I should have been looking at the thermometer. She had the kind of skin that doesn't need makeup. Her eyelashes were so long they should have their own zip code. And her hair bounced! My hair had never bounced. Tangled? Yes. Frizzed? Most definitely.

No. You will not get sucked into the swirling vortex that was the Cold Spell rumor mill. You will, however, buy a string bikini and wear it in Fiji.

This thought spiral was ridiculous and the direct result of my mother's rampant gossip. Valerie was not my enemy, and neither was her perfect hair.

"I think the goal marker is a great idea. You'll be over the top in no time. Which is what I wanted to talk to you about. Do you have a minute?"

"Can you hold that thought?" Valerie unclipped the radio at her hip. "I have to check in with the housekeeping staff first. We're busier than usual. Why don't we meet in the dining area in a half hour and then we'll talk?"

I nodded, clutching my notebook to my chest. Valerie capped the marker, then disappeared into a back room while I did a quick scan to make sure I wouldn't run into Leo. Confident the coast was clear, I went to the dining area and snagged a table partially hidden by a giant Christmas tree.

It was snowing again, gently, so I crossed my fingers, hoping it was flurries already predicted in the forecast. Snow could fall without it being some messed up curse.

With a menu hiding my face, and the tree blocking line of sight, I prepared to hunker down for the next thirty minutes. I was afraid if Leo found out about my imminent departure, he'd try to convince me to stay. Then again, if he *was* romantically interested in Valerie, he might hip-check me out of the picture and gladly let her take over. They'd cuddle up next to my notebook full of ideas and make out.

My heart squeezed. This was why I needed to leave. My brain was the only thing looking out for the scarred organ inside my chest. Otherwise, my heart was ready to throw caution to the wind and play in the snow, hoping Leo wouldn't slice his skis through it.

Thankfully, by the barest margin, my brain was still in charge.

The legs of the chair in front of me screeched across the hardwoods as someone slid into it. The scent of hot, greasy French fries hit my nose, and I peered over the edge of my menu, alarmed my brain had turned traitor too and was sending out brainwave signals alerting Leo to my location.

But it wasn't Leo. It was his best friend from high school, Aaron Jacobs. The man who'd witnessed my humiliation the night Leo never showed for our date. He stuffed a French fry in his mouth as two more chairs slid back and Blair and Gretchen, the most popular girls from school, joined my table.

They were the trio of my nightmares, transformed into full-blown adults. I didn't know if I was supposed to vault out of my chair before they hit me with a cutting remark, or greet them on common ground like we were old classmates who'd left the cliques of high school behind.

Unfortunately, because of my strategically placed spot at the table, the decision was made for me because I was literally stuck between a Christmas tree and a hard place.

"Sage Bennett, we thought that was you." Blair leaned in her chair, pulling me into one of those stiff hugs where we barely touched. She smelled like vanilla shampoo and wore a sleek ski jacket and a pair of form-fitting soft-shell ski pants.

"Hi," I said, frozen like a chipmunk in headlights.

Aaron grinned and ran a hand over his buzz-cut, then leaned back in the chair. "We wanted to come over because it's been a long time since we last saw you. You're the talk of the town."

"Yeah," Gretchen cut in. "It's good to see you, and we're glad you're here." She twisted a long brown lock of hair around her finger, flashing an expensive-looking gold bracelet studded with gemstones on her wrist. "We can't believe how we acted in high school. So petty, right? We're so embarrassed."

Was this a trap? It felt like a trap. Still, these were Leo's friends, and he'd come home looking for a clean slate. It was possible they felt remorse. The benefit of the doubt wouldn't kill me, and if this went south, it was another reason proving I should leave town. Frankly, my brain needed all the evidence it could get.

"You're right. That was a long time ago." I closed the menu and looked out the window. The snow was still light. We were good.

Blair touched my arm, and I tried not to flinch. Old habits die hard.

"Have some fries. It's a cheat day for me, otherwise, you'd never catch me eating fried food." Blair reached for a fry and nudged the basket closer. "Consider it a peace offering with a side of ketchup."

I chose a fry, reluctant to let my guard down, but it was fine. They didn't spill ketchup on my clothes or laugh and tell me they'd spoiled the food. We finished the basket while Aaron joked about the time he'd tried to impress a girl while skiing, only to find out she was an Olympic medalist.

Gretchen tossed her hair back and threw her napkin into the empty fry basket. "We should get going before the line at the lift gets too long. You know, Sage, the three of us have this tradition where we go to the top of the mountain and take a photo. You should join us. It's almost our five-year class reunion. Think about our photo on the big screen. Everyone will love it. We can catch up on the lift and ski down. It'll be fun."

I stuffed my hands in my coat pockets and shook my head, torn between apprehension and that feeling of being included by the cool crowd. I was surprised I'd recognized it. It had never happened before. *Must be a universal emotion.*

"I don't have the right clothes and I haven't skied in years. Maybe next time."

"Nonsense," Blair said. "It's like riding a bike, and I have an extra pair of ski pants. We're practically the same size." She eyed me with suspicion. "Are you doing Keto, too? Because you look incredible."

"No, I—"

"Then you have to tell us your secret." Blair wrapped her fingers around my wrist and pulled me up. The girls whisked me back to their guest room, and the next thing I knew, I was wearing ski pants and a pair of designer sunglasses that Blair decided fit the shape of my face.

Blair and Gretchen talked nonstop around me, and I realized I'd stepped through the looking glass into a bizarre version of my life where I was just one of the girls. Maybe it was wrong, but it felt good.

Aaron waited for us outside. He took a pair of rented skis off the rack and steadied me while I snapped into the bindings, then he slung a muscular arm over my shoulder.

"Ready, Sage? You're with me."

I tried to wriggle from under his arm, but the movement made me almost fall over my skis. He tightened his grip and teased me over losing my balance. The falling snow stuck to my face, and I blinked against the onslaught. I needed to relax and try to enjoy this moment. Not ruin it by letting old fears get in the way.

"Hey, Aaron!" I heard Leo's voice before I saw him.

I looked over my shoulder as Leo jogged toward us, his boots kicking up a layer of snow. His expression was dark, and he wasn't wearing a jacket as if he'd left the warmth of the lodge in a hurry.

"What's going on?" Leo's gaze dropped to my skis and his jaw tightened.

"We're taking Sage for a ski run. Don't worry, I'll pay for her lift ticket," Aaron said. He still had his arm around me.

Leo angled his head to the side and towed me out from under Aaron's grip. We stopped a few feet away, and I leaned against my ski poles as an icy wind sailed past.

"This isn't a good idea. I don't think you should go," he said.

"Why not? They're your friends."

He hesitated, shifting his gaze toward Aaron. There was a strange tension between the two of them. "Because you're out of practice, and I'm not able to go with you right now. I have a conference call I can't cancel. Give me an hour and I'll take you up."

"I'll be fine. I don't need a babysitter. We'll stick to the easy slopes."

"That's not what I mean. I'd feel better—"

Aaron skied over and clapped Leo on the back. "Hey, man, don't worry about Sage. I'll keep an eye on her for you. The girls think it will be fun to get some pictures at the top of the mountain like we always do, and then we can all get a drink at the bar. We'll save you a seat."

"Ooh, shots. Last one to the lift is buying!" Blair knocked her ski poles together, then dug them into the snow before pushing off toward the chairlift. Aaron shrugged as he and Gretchen raced after her.

Leo held my arm, keeping me from skiing toward the lift. "Just be careful. Promise me you'll stay off the black diamond trails."

I brushed off his concern, poking him in the ribs. "No fair. You're making me last. Now I have to buy drinks for your friends. Will you be happy if I promise to purchase top-shelf liquor?"

He ground his teeth. "The trails, Bennett. Promise me that."

"Fine. Don't worry so much. You taught me everything I know, remember?" I pushed off with my skis, then called over my shoulder. "Tell Valerie I'll meet her after our run. Oh, and

I left my notebook under the reservation desk. It has all my notes, so don't throw it out unless you want an extremely angry witch on your hands."

Gretchen and Blair caught the first lift, leaving me with Aaron. I grabbed onto the side of the chair as it lifted us off the ground, making my stomach lurch. I hated heights. The lift was a necessary evil, but I had never liked it, certain I'd fall off and end up in a mangled pile of skis and snow.

We climbed higher, my stomach knotting at the nearly thirty-foot drop.

"Whatever you do, don't shake the chair."

Aaron laughed. But this time, it was a low sound that made the back of my neck prickle.

"What? Like this?" He rocked forward in the seat, shifting his weight until the chair jolted. "Are you scared? You won't fall." He shook the chair again, seeming to take pleasure in my fear. I closed my eyes and held on. Leo might have been right. This was a bad idea.

Aaron leaned against me, crowding me to the edge of the chair. His heavy breath assailed my neck. "So, you and Leo are close again, huh? I'm surprised."

"Why's that?" I asked as the chair shuddered along the cable, cresting the tops of the trees. A cold feeling sank into my bones. I forced a smile and waved when Blair and Gretchen turned in their seat to look back at us.

"After what happened with you two, I assumed you'd stay away." He angled his head closer. "People don't change much, you know?"

Yeah, I was starting to believe it.

"I don't want you to get the wrong idea all over again. It's nothing personal. It's just the way it is."

"No. I'm only helping Leo while I'm in town. I'm leaving soon. This week, in fact."

"Good." Aaron flashed his teeth. "Then we can have some fun while we're here. Who knows when we'll get another chance?"

The falling snow kicked into gear, and I brushed a layer off my ski pants when the lift reached the top. I stood as we hit the platform and skied down the small hill, following the two girls as they veered right.

They sailed past a group of trail signs, then twisted abruptly into a parallel stop, sending a wave of white powder into the air.

"I think the easier trails are that way," I said, pointing with my pole.

"No, there's a beginner trail that cuts through this section. It has an amazing view. We usually take our picture there." Blair adjusted her goggles and angled her head toward a trail running through the trees. "Follow us."

I weighed my options. I could go back the way we came and try to ski for the first time in ages all alone, or I could finish the run with them and head home when it was over. I definitely wasn't staying for a drink. Aaron had let his friendly mask slip on the lift. I didn't want to be around when he took it off completely.

"Come on! It's this way," Gretchen shouted before she skied through the trees.

I huffed an icy breath and slid my skis forward. Twenty minutes and I'd be back at the lodge.

They waited for me in front of a trail sign after I slowed to a stop. Two black diamonds and the words, experts only, were painted on the sign. A dusting of snow obscured the trail name, but I didn't need to read it to know it was ominous.

"I thought we were sticking with green circles." I blocked the snow from my face and peeked over the ledge. It looked like a straight drop with moguls, funneling into a sharp turn leading deeper down the trail.

"Oh, please." Blair curled her lip into a sneer. "If you wanted to take it easy, you shouldn't have left the bunny slope. Wait—didn't you take lessons with a bunch of children? That's so lame. I think you need a new nickname." Blair tapped her finger against her chin. "How about...Sage the Baby Mage."

Gretchen let out bitter laugh. "What's lame is thinking you can come home after a few years and think you're one of us."

I recoiled, pushing back on my skis to create distance. My throat burned. I should have known better. This was all a nasty trick. People don't change. They get meaner.

"You look upset. Are you going to put a hex on me?" Blair taunted, crossing her ski poles like she was trying to ward me away.

Aaron skied between us and gave me a hard look before angling toward the slope. "Come on, let's leave her here. The snow's getting worse. We've had our fun. I'm ready for a drink."

He took off down the slope, maneuvering expertly over the steep terrain, then vanished into the blinding snow.

"I guess we'll see you at the bottom...or not. Remember to point your skis into a V and make a snowplow." Blair's lips trembled as she tried to restrain her laughter. She motioned to Gretchen and the two of them left me standing at the top of the slope.

I wiped away the snow pelting my face. The flakes melted and mixed with the tears stinging the corners of my eyes. I swallowed a sob and felt my chest shudder. Now wasn't the time to cry. Tears wouldn't get me through this. They'd only make the snow worse.

So much for my sunny stretch. The curse was back. Had it ever left? Maybe it was bidding its time, letting me think a little self-care and a moving speech in the town square was enough to break the spell.

I tipped my skis toward the edge. There was no turning back. I had to figure it out on my own. *Just go slow, make a V.* I closed my eyes and imagined Leo standing next to me, coaching me down the hill. *You got this, Bennett. I'll pick you up if you fall.*

Oh, I was going to fall. A lot. But I would pick myself up and get the heck out of Cold Spell.

A wall of wind and ice slammed into my face as if the storm had laughed and shouted back, "You're staying right here!"

I slid a few inches at a time, scraping my skis against the hard-packed snow. My stomach twisted in knots and little dots danced in front of my eyes. I forced myself to focus, deep breaths, then slid a few more feet.

My skis slipped out from underneath me, and I landed hard, coasting a distance on my butt. It hurt, but it counted as progress. I stood back up and tried again.

This time, I made it about thirty feet before I fell. At this rate, I'd be here all night.

How long does it take to freeze to death? Probably just enough time to give me a shot at meeting the Grim Reaper. I clenched my teeth. I would not die on this mountain and have my obituary on the front page of the Gazette.

The article would read: *She had a good run, winning a prestigious award. Then she died tragically at the hands of her high school bullies. Who went on to live an envied life of wealth and success. We never did get that photo of her award.*

I scowled and clicked out of my skis. Forget this. I'd walk the rest of the way and someone could come back for my skis later. At least I wouldn't break my neck.

Using my poles, I climbed to my feet and took my first couple of steps. The going was clunky in ski boots but manageable.

The snow had developed into a ferocious blizzard, falling in sheets of ice. I shivered and kept going, walking for what felt like hours without making much progress. No one else skied past, and with the weather like this, I was sure they had closed the lifts.

I was alone on the mountain. An allegory for what had amounted to my life.

Things were *not* fine or fantastic.

I pushed onward until a strange sound made me stop. Turning my head, I listened to the wind. Was that a crack? Another jagged sound sent fear spiking through my chest.

Looking back, I watched in horror as a section of snow broke free and barreled down the mountain straight toward me.

Chapter 11

Leo

I paced in front of my office window, watching the snow. The storm that started as a few flakes had progressed into nearly white-out conditions. An hour had passed since Sage went up the chairlift, and I told Valerie to let me know once she made it back to the lodge. So far, Valerie hadn't radioed in.

"I'm going to have to call you back. There's an emergency," I said into the phone, ending the conference call early.

A bad feeling twisted in my gut. I shouldn't have let Aaron and the other girls take Sage up the mountain. But what was I supposed to do? Embarrass her by hauling her over my shoulder, and then tying her to the chair in my office so I could keep my eyes on her?

It sounded like a sane plan now that the snow was flying and my adrenaline raced because she hadn't returned. But before, it was only a jealous instinct crossed with mistrust over their intentions.

Aaron and I weren't friends. Not for a long time.

I grabbed the radio and left my office, walking through the staff area of the lodge until I entered the lobby. A few guests milled through the area and warmed their hands by the fire.

Shouts and laughter erupted from the dining area, and I headed for it, hoping to see Sage sitting at the bar doing shots and laughing over the group photo they'd taken at the top of the mountain.

I scanned the groups of people, spotting Aaron and the two others at a table in the corner. A half-filled pitcher of beer sat in front of them, and they clinked glasses, then chugged back the brew.

"Did you see her face?" Blair said, mopping up a puddle of beer she'd drunkenly spilled with her napkin. "She really thought we wanted to hang out."

My footsteps paused, hearing the ridicule in Blair's voice, confirming my worst fears. I wrapped my hands around the back of her chair and squared my jaw.

"Where is Sage?"

Gretchen snickered, then hiccuped. "She's probably still on the trail."

I glared at Aaron. "You left her up there? The weather turned. It's dangerous. What were you thinking?"

"She'll be fine, Leo. Chill. You always get so uptight over that girl. She's not like us."

"I know." I snapped. "That's a good thing. What trail did you take?"

Aaron rose from his seat and rounded the table. He hooked his thumbs into his belt buckles and smirked. "The Gauntlet."

"A double black diamond? You're such a jerk, Aaron."

He scoffed. "I'm the jerk? You think you're so much better than us. I'll bet you still haven't told Sage what your father made you do." He stepped closer, jutting his chin in my face, nostrils flaring. "How do you think she'd feel if she knew the truth about you and your family, and the lengths you'd go to hurt people?"

A red haze blurred my vision. "Get out. All of you." I gritted my teeth and pointed toward the exit. "Get your bags and get off my mountain. If you're not gone by the time I get back, I won't need to call security. I'll throw you out myself."

I left as Aaron sputtered, and the girls whined about finishing their drinks. I grabbed my gear and skis from the locker, spotting Valerie as she rushed into the patrol office.

"Good, you're here," she said, shrugging into her jacket and following me outside. "I think Sage is still somewhere on the mountain. We already closed the lifts and ski patrol is out clearing the trails, making sure everyone gets back safely." Valerie chewed on her lip, worry in her eyes. "This storm came out of nowhere."

"I know. I'm going to find her. She's on The Gauntlet. I'll radio if I need help."

"Be careful, Leo. That's a nasty trail. Especially in this weather."

I nodded, but I didn't need the reminder. It was our toughest slope. Sage wouldn't have been ready for it on a sunny day, let alone in this mess.

My hands clenched around my ski poles, but I would have preferred they were clenched around Aaron's neck.

I skied toward the lift while the attendant got it running. The ride up was a method of torture; the chair juddering slowly through the wind-driven snow. I tensed with the sway of the lift, trying not to imagine every hazardous pitfall Sage might have encountered.

This was my fault. I manipulated her into helping me and then left her with those idiots, still obsessed with childish pranks. I knew better. Had witnessed how some people treated her when we were younger. She shouldn't have had to experience it then, and especially not now when I should have protected her.

Aaron was right about one thing, though. I wasn't some innocent bystander in our past, and if she found out what had happened years ago, she'd never speak to me again. After this, maybe she shouldn't.

I exited the lift and skied toward the trail, keeping low against the howling wind. Snow pummeled my goggles and made visibility a challenge. My heart rattled behind my rib cage and a sick feeling gnawed at my insides.

The trail they'd taken came into view, and I scanned the area, then slanted over the ledge, dropping onto the sheer face of the slope. My skis screeched across the ice before hitting loose powder, jarring my knees. The moguls were rough and barely visible, forcing me to expect the dips and brace against the impact.

A pair of skis appeared on the edge of the trail, and I swerved to a stop. They were rentals and looked like the pair Sage had worn.

"Good girl," I murmured, making sure she wasn't waiting on the side of the trail. She'd taken off her skis instead of trying to battle the slope. Walking wouldn't be easy, but she'd have more control.

Leaving the skis behind, I continued down the trail. My eyes tracked back and forth, careful I didn't miss her. I squinted, spotting a bright-colored jacket against the wall of white. Sage was in the distance and she had looked back up the mountain.

I raised my ski pole, thinking she'd spotted me when I heard the sound. The breath froze in my lungs. A whoosh filled the air as a section of snow let loose, sliding straight toward her.

It happened so fast. Sage reacted, first trying to run, then she veered toward the edge of the trail, lunging to avoid the rushing snow. She didn't make it far enough, and the avalanche clipped her legs, knocking her to the ground. She wasn't moving as the snow settled.

I sucked in a breath, only remembering to breathe when my lungs seized. My mouth was dry, nerves shot as I leaned forward, letting my skis slice through the loose snow.

It was difficult to balance, and only years on the slopes and experience as an instructor kept me upright. I reached Sage in under a minute and clicked out of my skis, boots sinking in the deep snow.

She still hadn't moved, and I scrambled on my knees to her side.

"Sage?" Panic laced my voice. I bent over her, brushing snow from her face. My throat ached, and I didn't recognize the hoarse sound breaking the silence. "Bennett, wake up."

She winced, blinking open her eyes with a soft moan.

"Leo? Is that you?"

Relief exploded in my chest, nearly making me dizzy. I rested my hands on her shoulders, preventing her from sitting up.

"Yeah, it's me. Don't move yet. Just breathe for a second. Do you hurt anywhere?" I asked, gently running my hands over her limbs to check for broken bones.

"I don't think so. Wait, yes, my head hurts. I think I used it to break my fall." A weak smile warmed her lips.

I ran my fingers behind her head, carefully searching for bruises. Then I checked her pupils. Normal, as far as I could tell.

"Who told you to do that?" I rasped, finally helping her sit up.

"I couldn't land on my butt. It was too bruised from my previous falls. Gotta spread the wealth." She gazed past me at the trail. "Did I start an avalanche?"

"Sort of. It was only a size one. They call it a sluff. Enough snow to knock you off your feet, but not enough to bury you."

"You're such a ski nerd," she grumbled, her eyes narrowing as she focused back on me. "Are you minimizing my avalanche? Because that's a slippery slope."

I let out a rusty laugh and cupped the side of her face with my glove. "No. I support all avalanche sizes. I'm very pro-snow."

She snorted. "Don't make me laugh. It hurts."

My thumb brushed over her cheek. The ache in my throat was back, and I tried to clear it away. "I know, Bennett. I'm going to get you fixed up."

I pulled out my radio and requested ski patrol. Then gave out our location.

Her nose wrinkled. "You're going to make me go down the hill in one of those sleds, aren't you? That's so embarrassing. Do I have to?"

"You have a possible head injury. You get the sled. Don't fight me on this. I own the place."

She nodded with a slight pout, then visibly swallowed. "Thanks for coming, Grayson."

"Anytime, Bennett." The words came out softer than I'd intended, laced with a feeling I was struggling to keep buried.

I shifted positions, allowing her to lie back down, her head resting in my lap as we waited for the ski patrol.

The snow had eased, falling gently in huge flakes in an almost dreamlike quality. A quiet hush fell over the trail as the wind stilled, and it seemed the worst of the storm had passed. But as Sage snuggled deeper in my lap, a different storm battered relentlessly inside my chest, and it was only getting started.

Chapter 12

Sage

The light was dim when I opened my eyes. My muscles ached, and my head had a dull throb, but I was warm, and wrapped in a thick blanket. I wrinkled my brow, noticing the distinct lack of popstar posters on the ceiling. I was not in my bedroom, and this was definitely not a twin bed.

That's right. I started an avalanche. Leo had called it a sluff—but for anyone who asked, I would call it, 'the big one.'

I rolled carefully onto my side, tucking the blanket under my chin, and realized I wasn't alone. Leo was asleep in a chair he'd pulled close to the bed. His head rested on his shoulder, legs crossed at the knee. Frown lines marred his forehead as if he were having a bad dream.

Maybe that was all this was—a dream. I'd wake up Monday morning, alarm clock blaring, walls shaking as the train rumbled past on the tracks near my apartment. I'd shuffle into the office, coffee in hand, and read over my next case file. Other people's miracles waited. My life was exactly the way I'd left it.

So then why did I clutch the blanket tighter, staring at Leo, afraid to even blink in case the room around me vanished?

It was dark outside the window, nighttime creeping in while I'd slept. Leo must have sensed me wake because he caught me watching him. For a long moment, neither of us spoke. The weight of his gaze made everything else blur like a shaken snow globe, and I soaked it in, reluctant to break the spell.

"Hi," I whispered.

"Hey." He leaned forward, concern etching his features. "How do you feel?"

I stretched out my legs, pointing my toes to test the twinge in my muscles. "Honestly? Like I won the mattress lottery. Who knew an upgrade was a ski accident away? I would have bought a lift ticket the day I arrived."

Leo's lips twitched. "I meant your head. But I'm pleased you're satisfied with the lodge's memory foam density."

"Is this your room?" I asked, suddenly less interested in the mattress than the window into his private domain.

Leo had thrown a sweater over the back of an armchair, next to a small table holding a well-worn novel. An older pair of skis leaned against the wall, alongside a pair of boots. The bindings were unclipped. There were no framed photographs or family pictures. Only a glossy panoramic view of the mountain taken from an overlook spot sitting on a shelf.

It was strange how a room could be both cozy and lonely at the same time.

"Yes," he answered, oblivious to my inspection. "I've been staying at the lodge. It's convenient and cheaper until I can get a place of my own. I hope you don't mind that I put you in here. Medical checked your head injury—no concussion, thankfully—and gave you something for the pain. It knocked you out pretty quickly. You've been asleep for hours. I called your parents. They know you're staying here tonight." He paused. "And you don't have to worry about Aaron and the other two. They're gone."

I nodded and closed my eyes, but all I saw were Blair and Gretchen's mocking sneers. I blinked them away. "I'm sorry about what happened. I should have listened to you and told them no. It was stupid of me to think they'd changed."

"It wasn't stupid, and it's not your fault. I wish I could have done more than just kick them out."

"But they're your friends."

"Not anymore." A laugh rumbled under his breath. "You should have seen it. I told them to get off my mountain. It was intoxicating. I think the power might go to my head. Where's the line between villain and mega-villain?"

I smiled softly. "I think it's more of a gray area."

"Shady and mysterious. That tracks."

I struggled to sit up and winced as pain spiked in my temple. The amusement vanished from Leo's face, replaced with a quiet intensity that caught me off guard. He leaned forward to help adjust my pillow.

His scent wrapped around me, and I let my eyes drift shut for a moment. This time, all I saw was his steady hand as he helped me out of the snow, and the way he'd lightly brushed the flakes from my hair while we waited for ski patrol.

My breath caught when I felt Leo's fingers graze my cheek. Agonizingly slow, like ice melting on warm skin. He made a rough sound in the back of his throat, checking himself, then pulled away to curl his hand into a loose fist.

His withdrawal left me feeling off balance. I was caught between wanting more and the fear that if I got my wish, it might all be an illusion. After today, I didn't know what was real anymore or if I could trust myself to figure it out.

Leo pushed out of his chair and paced in front of the bed.

"Are you hungry?" he asked, spinning to find his room key. He tucked it into his pocket and opened the door. "I'll go get you something to eat. Relax...or feel free to snoop in my medicine cabinet. I already hid all the embarrassing stuff."

He grinned, slipping back into his playful banter, only to wince and shake his head before closing the door. I waited until his footsteps faded down the hall. While the medicine cabinet was tempting, there was something I needed to take care of first.

My phone sat on the coffee table, and I hobbled out of bed to collect it. Time to face facts. My weather curse wasn't broken, and I didn't have any clue how to fix it. I thought helping Leo would stop the snow, but it seemed to have no effect. A job well done had not brought clear skies. It had only made my feelings murkier.

I was still a liability in the agency's eyes, and they weren't going to let me work on my next case. I'd run out of time, and while I wouldn't be fulfilling miracles in Wood Pine, there was still a miracle I could grant.

I typed the message, asking to name my replacement. I wrote a bulleted list of all the reasons Delia was ready, leaving out that it was the prophesied word of a questionable fortune teller. Though now that I thought about it, maybe there was something there.

With a satisfied crack of my knuckles, I hit send.

Ten minutes later, my phone jingled with the message: *Request granted.*

I sank into the armchair, pulling Leo's sweater into my lap for warmth. My life was still a mess, and I was stuck in Cold Spell for a while longer, but this was the right thing to do. Delia deserved the chance to prove herself.

Now all I had to do was call her and deliver the good news.

Chapter 13

Leo

"You look tired," Valerie said, glancing up from her spreadsheet. She clicked to close the document and sat on the edge of my desk with her arms folded.

"I slept on the sofa in the staff breakroom," I said, rolling my neck to relieve the tension. It felt like there was a vice around my shoulders and nothing eased it.

"That was three days ago."

Right. Three days. And I've hardly slept since. I could blame it on the resort being busier than ever, but really, it was that freaking mattress.

No, the memory foam density was fine. It was the fact Sage had slept on it, and now the whole bed smelled like her. Even after washing the sheets, so it was definitely psychological. *Candy cane sugar mixed with the lingering scent of sugared berries.* A fatal combination. I was a goner. Might as well switch rooms because there were no other options.

"Have you tried asking Sage out on a date?" Valerie asked, bluntly.

"What? No. I can't do that." I scrubbed a hand over my jaw and corrected myself. "I mean, why would I do that? We're just friends...kind of."

"Wow!" Valerie dropped her head into her hand and rubbed the spot above her eyebrow. "As your festive minion, I'm disappointed with your lack of self-awareness, not to mention your level of defeat." She pushed off the desk and jabbed her finger in my face. "Where is the man willing to put on a mortifying elf costume? What happened to the quest for Cold Spell domination through a cleverly disguised blackmail plot, leading to your second shot at romance? Have I taught you nothing?"

Her words landed like a snowball to the back of the head. "Second shot at romance? Have you been paying attention? My ex-friends terrorized her on my mountain. She was almost injured in a very small—yet not insignificant avalanche. And that's not even getting into the fact she hates me for what I did to her all those years ago. It's not a lack of self-awareness. Trust me. I'm *extremely* aware I have no chance of fixing this."

Valerie huffed and sank back down on the edge of the desk. Her fingers tapped out a rhythm on the wooden surface. "Okay. I see your point. This is a tricky situation, and it requires deep thought." She chewed on the corner of her mouth for a minute, then snapped her fingers. "I know. We need to act like ninjas and sneak attack. Are you familiar with the use of a grappling hook?"

I groaned. With Valerie in charge, I was going to die alone in a botched rappelling accident.

"Absolutely not. Will you stop devising weird plans where I have to think like a villain or act like a ninja? Where do you come up with this stuff?"

Valerie shrugged. "It's in the handbook."

"What handbook?"

"That's not important."

I squeezed my eyes shut, counted to three, then planted my fists on the desk. "How about, I do something normal like take her somewhere quiet where the two of us can talk?"

Valerie picked at her cuticle and sniffed. "It's not as cinematic, but it has an appeal. Okay!" She rallied, clapping her hands like she was breaking a huddle. "I'll lure Sage to the lodge and you trigger your mundane talking idea. May I suggest snacks? Maybe a bottle of red?"

"No. I'll handle the details. You finish up the plans for our last fundraiser. We still have a sizable amount of money to raise. I want to see Sage's face when we cross the threshold. It'll mean a lot to her."

"Got it. I'll handle the fundraiser." Valerie collected the notebook Sage had left behind. "You don't have to worry about a thing. Your talking plan is solid. No one ever fell asleep while someone was talking."

"Valerie," I warned.

She held up her hands. "The truth shall set you free. But if it doesn't, and it blows up in your face like an inflatable lawn Santa, maybe improvise a little." Valerie wriggled her eyebrows suggestively. "Sometimes a guy just needs to take action."

The ski lift shuddered to life, grinding its gears as the chairs began a slow climb up the mountain.

Morning sunlight bounced off the snow, and the frigid air was sharp in my lungs. I stood behind Sage, arms tense to catch her if she spun around and charged back to the lodge.

"There is no way you're getting me back on that thing." Sage eyed the lift like it was the Abominable Snowman. She folded her arms and dug in her heels. "Keep dreaming, Grayson."

"Come on, Bennett. I already promised we weren't going to ski. You're wearing regular boots." Placing my palms on her shoulders, I nudged her toward the lift. "This is strictly a scenic outing. Where is your adventurous spirit?"

"My spirit was almost exorcised by a sweeping avalanche. I'm still having nightmares. I may never sleep again."

"Me either," I muttered as a burst of wind carried with it the scent of mint and berries. She walked a few steps closer to the lift, and I squeezed her shoulders. "It'll be fine. You can't run away from the mountain just because you had a bad fall."

Sage scoffed as she allowed me to guide her onto a moving chair. "Don't use your ski nerd wisdom on me. I'm in your rickety excuse for an escalator, aren't I? People are not meant to dangle over the treetops by a wire. If I die, put that on my tombstone. Tell the world my story."

The chair lifted off the ground, and she yelped. I buried a smile and lowered the safety bar.

We climbed the first few minutes in silence, Sage holding onto the side of the lift with a death grip. Every time the chair bounced, her features grew paler. I leaned forward to adjust my position.

"Don't move!" Sage's fingers dug into my knee.

"You're safe, Bennett," I said, covering her hand with mine. "Nothing bad will happen. Trust me. Now, come here." I raised my arm along the back of the chair, opening a space in the crook of my shoulder.

She seemed to calculate my offer, the wind speed, and whether the slightest movement might send us crashing to the ground. Finally, she nodded and inched into my side. Her muscles relaxed one by one as I draped my arm around her. A tiny sigh escaped her lips, and I tightened my hold, the air thinning in my chest. The best plan of my life had my emotions frayed and ready to snap.

"Better?" I asked, my chin resting near the top of her head. Wisps of her hair tickled my nose.

"Ask me again when I'm on the ground." She snuggled closer, tucking her gloved hands against my chest. "What's in the bag?"

"A surprise."

"You're very vague and mysterious. Being a villain has changed you."

I smiled into her hair. "Nah. I'm still the same." My voice dipped, filling with rust. "Some things haven't changed at all."

"That's what scares me," she whispered so quietly I wasn't sure she meant for me to hear.

The lift rumbled to the top of the slope and I waved to the lift attendant as we disembarked.

"We're going down the same way, right?" Sage asked, craning her neck toward the chairs revolving back down the mountain.

"Oh, now you want to ride the lift," I teased. I snaked an arm around her middle and led her away from the main group of ski trails.

"Only because it's efficient. Not because it was enjoyable."

Her eyes glinted with humor. At least her fear was gone. I'd have to settle for lukewarm compliments until I could get the real thing. We walked a little further, detouring through a lightly wooded area. The snow crunched under our boots, untouched by others. It was quiet. Peaceful. No interruptions.

"Where are you taking me? Seriously, if you pull out a blindfold, I'm not taking another step." Sage balled her fists on her hips as I bent to pull back a giant fir branch.

"Then you'll miss the view."

I heard her sharp inhale as the landscape came into focus. Giant snow-capped peaks shimmered in the distance. The sky was a crisp blue, and a heavy fog blanketed the lower slopes, revealing the tips of pine trees. It was a view you could stare at for hours. Never changing. Always steadfast.

No matter how far away you run, it would still be here waiting to welcome you back.

"There's not even a cloud in the sky," Sage murmured, tilting her head to allow the sunlight to catch her face.

"Come with me. I want to show you something else." I guided Sage toward an enclosed outlook nearly hidden by the trees. The building was narrow, consisting of a platform behind a wall of giant windows. It was neglected with a few holes in the roof and had no electricity, but it was built on a sturdy foundation.

The door creaked open as we entered, and Sage wandered toward the expanse of windows. I removed a key from the zippered pocket in my bag and unlocked a closet containing an emergency kit, blankets, and a battery-powered heater.

Dragging out the blankets and the heater, I turned the battery on and placed it on the floor. "We won't have beach weather with this thing, but it will take the chill off."

"Darn. So much for the bikini I have on under this winter gear." Sage removed her gloves and sat cross-legged while I handed her a thermos.

"Suddenly, I regret not taking you to the Polar Bear Plunge."

She laughed softly and unscrewed the cap on the thermos. Her eyes drifted to half-mast as she breathed in the steam. "Peppermint hot chocolate. An underrated flavor, but it's my favorite."

"Don't forget this." I handed her a candy cane from my bag. She twisted off the plastic and dunked it into the thermos, giving the drink a quick stir.

The room continued to warm as I joined her on the floor. We removed our thick jackets, settling in to enjoy our drinks and a rare stillness.

"So what is all this, Leo?" She waved a hand around the room. But there was a note in her voice, making me think she was asking about something deeper.

"This is phase two of the renovation. It needs a lot of work, and an addition, and extensive electrical work. But I think this place could make a great ski-in cafe. What do you think?"

"It has a beautiful view, and people will love it. I think it's a great idea. How long have you known about this place?"

"A long time. I used to come up here by myself when I first came on as a ski instructor. I had to sneak in because it was off-limits, but I needed a place to escape all the noise. My father was tough—well, you know—and his expectations and control forced me to find a spot where I could be away from it all. This mountain became that place for me."

"How come you never told me? We used to meet up after every lesson, usually until the lifts closed. You never said anything."

"Because after I met you, I didn't need to come up here anymore."

"Leo..." She dropped her gaze, staring at her marshmallows. "I miss those days, too."

Now. Tell her the truth now.

"Sage, I—"

But she lifted her head before I could finish, a burden weighing behind her eyes. "Leo, can I tell you something I haven't told anyone else?"

"Of course."

"This is so humiliating. You already know I never won the agency award. But the truth is, they put me on a forced sabbatical too. I was messing up at work, stressed out, and not feeling like myself. I haven't felt like myself in a long time. And that's when the snow started."

"What do you mean?"

"My family has this strange curse. It causes weather-related incidents whenever we're dealing with something troubling or our life isn't going the way we planned. My curse manifests snow. The agency thinks I'm a liability, so they reassigned my cases and sent me home. I can't stop the storms, and I can't figure out what's causing them. Coming back here was supposed to fix it, but it only seems to be making things worse. I don't know what to do, and I'm scared that if I can't stop the snow, I'll lose everything."

My stomach sank. This was because of me—and maybe that was arrogant to think—but I'd forced my way back into Sage's life because it was what I needed. What I wanted. I should have been helping her, not the other way around.

Valerie's words echoed in my mind. *The truth will set you free...* But I'd already ruined things between us once. Telling her the truth about what happened back then would only add to her worries. It was selfish—*and I wanted to be selfish*. More than I wanted to win over the town. More than I wanted to save the resort.

I wanted Sage.

But not if it hurt her. Not if it made me more like my father.

Sage shook her head. "So I'm stuck here until I figure it out. But I'm glad you showed me this place. It hasn't snowed once today. Maybe this is what I needed."

Or maybe I almost ruined your chance to break the curse by telling you the truth.

The radio crackled in my bag. Valerie's muffled voice came over the line.

"You should answer that. There might be an emergency back at the lodge." Sage pointed to my bag with her candy cane as Valerie spoke again.

Pulling out the radio, I pressed the talk button. "This is Leo. What's going on? Over."

"You won't believe what happened. Over."

I glanced at Sage, listening from her spot on the floor. "Valerie, now is not a good time. Over."

"But I have news. You said you wanted to know when we raised enough money. We just got an anonymous donation for the rest of the project. We're fully funded! Let Sage know. Over and out."

The radio went quiet in my hand, and I stared at it, stunned. Who would donate such a large sum of money? And why do it anonymously?

"Leo, is what Valerie said true? We're fully funded?"

The floorboards creaked as Sage came up behind me. I put the radio back in my bag, and when I faced her, I only had a second to think before she slipped into my arms. A wide smile spread across her lips as she tilted her head to look at me.

"I can't believe we did it! Leo, this is incredible."

Her fingers tangled in my shirt. Her heart beating against mine.

"This only happened because of you," I said, my resolve slipping enough to make me pull her closer. Let my fingers press into her back. I allowed myself to be selfish for a moment, hoping it would last for a lifetime.

But her eyes softened, melting into something that made my chest tighten. Time stalled, then sped up double time as she wet her lips, her teeth scraping the delicate skin. Sage lifted on her toes, inching closer. It was the longest wait of my life for the thing I wanted most.

I didn't pull away because I knew I'd regret it one way or another. Regret that I'd never had the chance to kiss her or regret that it only happened once. Was there a lesser evil?

She pressed her lips softly to mine.

Just one kiss. Only a villain would take more.

But as she opened up to me, filling my senses, and making me desperate, I realized she was wrong about one thing. There was no gray area between a villain and a mega-villain. There was a hard line. And my hands cupped her face, pushing her back against the windows as I crossed it.

Chapter 14
Sage

The window felt cold against my back, but the rest of me was on fire. Leo pressed his body into my hips, keeping me still as his mouth slanted over mine. Again and again. *As if I'd run away from this.*

His fingers threaded through my hair, tugging gently, fisting the strands as if that alone could release some of the smoldering tension. I sucked in a breath as his lips moved, trailing down my neck, creating a deliberate path of sensation I felt everywhere. This wasn't what I'd imagined when I decided to kiss him, caught in the moment, hearing what we'd accomplished together.

I thought it might be sweet. Even satisfying after so many years of wanting him. This was so much more.

It felt like something inside of me clicking into place for the first time in my life. A puzzle piece that had fallen on the floor, and I'd searched for it, certain I'd never be complete. That it was gone forever. Until now.

I was terrified, utterly, and totally that this moment might not be real, and all the pieces would scatter to the wind.

But he made me believe. He'd been putting my heart back together ever since I arrived home.

His mouth found mine again, almost blistering, and then something happened. A rough sound rumbled in his throat and he bit back a curse. His fingers loosened, and cold air rushed into the space he allowed between our bodies.

I blinked, scrambling to figure out what I'd done; my throat too tight to ask. Leo pressed his forehead against mine. Air rushed out of his lungs and he grit his teeth.

"Sage, I can't do this."

The words made me freeze. My entire body turned to ice, but my mind reeled. *No. This isn't happening. Not again.*

"I'm sorry," he choked. "This isn't right. I never should have—"

My hands shoved against his chest, forcing him back, but not far enough. I searched his eyes, the edges of my vision blurring with tears at the pained look reflecting at me.

"Why?" I asked, silently begging him to explain. If there was a reason, I could make sense of this. He had to feel something for me. You don't kiss your enemies like that. Or maybe you do. What did I know? Maybe that was what made people enemies—experiencing a kiss that life-changing, knowing you'll never capture it again.

He refused to look at me. His agonized silence filled the room, a mockery of the peaceful stillness outside. The stunning mountain, and this moment I thought was our second chance.

I had to go. I couldn't stay here. Whatever explanation he had, he wasn't giving it. My legs were numb as I searched for my jacket, then blindly put it on. The zipper snagged in the teeth, refusing to budge. I jerked my arm to make it work, a sob burning in my chest.

"Let me help you."

"No." I dropped the zipper and snatched my gloves. "Getting close to you again was a mistake."

Leo reached for me, his voice breaking. "Don't say that. Please, Bennett. Just don't say that."

I backed toward the door. "You have the money for the rink now. You got what you wanted."

"That's not what this is about." His hands scrubbed through his hair, and he squeezed his eyes shut before trying to answer. "I know you don't understand, but I never wanted to hurt you. Ever."

A harsh laugh escaped the rawness of my throat. "I can't believe I fell for this again. We're done, Leo. For good, this time. Our deal is over. Tell people whatever you want about me. And best of luck with the resort. I'm sure it will be a huge success. Now that you're the golden boy again."

My boots sank into the deep snow as I bolted back to the lift. I was such a fool, thinking things were different. That maybe I'd been wrong about before. A strange part of me had believed there was more to our past, and if I figured out what it was, it would fix everything.

The sky had grown overcast and giant flakes fell as I ran away from Leo for the second time in my life.

Let it snow. Because I wasn't going back.

***

"This might be the snowiest Christmas on record," my mother said as she arranged a pine garland twisted with fairy lights around the linen-draped banquet table.

I didn't need to look outside to know she was right. It had been a week since I left Leo standing by the overlook, and the storms were coming one after another. Some were quick squalls of angry flakes, others were gentle, almost dreamlike. No matter what I did. No matter how many times I tried to relax—or attempted to numb the pain for a night with spiked eggnog—the snow kept coming.

"I hope the weather doesn't keep people away from our event." My mother opened a container of finger sandwiches and placed each one on a metal-tiered display. "It's wonderful the rink project is funded, but your father is so excited to show off his latest recipe. We're thinking about adding some new items to the tea menu."

I stole a finger sandwich from the box and pressed the spongy bread lightly between my fingers before taking a bite. Since we'd raised enough money for the rink project, thanks to the help from an anonymous donor, the money raised from tonight's party would go to a local charity. With only three days until Christmas, the turnout was expected to be huge as the town gathered to celebrate the holiday.

The lodge's great room had been transformed into a festive winter wonderland with crystal ornaments hanging from the exposed beams and white vintage lantern centerpieces casting a warm glow over the tables. Extra staff put the final touch on the decorations, lighting pillar candles, and preparing for the guests to arrive. There was no sign of Leo.

We hadn't spoken since that day on the mountain. It was what I wanted, but I couldn't stop the hopeful part of me that jumped every time my phone jingled with a text. I might be on a forced sabbatical, but if this were one of my cases, I would be in the trenches, working like mad to bring my couple back together. But magical agents weren't working behind the scenes for me, and as we inched closer to Christmas, the thought of a miracle made me want to sink my phone into a holiday Jell-O mold and sleep till New Year's.

Fifteen more minutes, and I would make my escape, vanishing into the arriving crowd like a magician in a puff of smoke. Valerie had taken over the main hosting duties, and I was merely a part of the setup crew. Back home, there was a bag of popcorn and the scary version of *A Christmas Carol* with my name on it. No more holiday rom-coms for me. They weren't hitting the same.

"All right, everyone, it's almost time to get this party started!" Valerie walked into the room wearing a long, black dress and giant snowflake earrings that sparkled with each step.

She'd replaced her trusty radio with an earpiece, and she pressed her finger to the device, speaking softly. I didn't need to guess who was on the other end of that mic.

Make that ten minutes until departure.

"Sage, You're here!" Valerie flashed a thumbs up to a tray of appetizers and nodded her approval at the centerpieces before she joined me by the banquet tables. "And you look amazing. I love your dress."

I smoothed my palms down the strapless, red velvet cocktail dress that skimmed the middle of my thighs and fit like a second skin over my body. I'd learned my lesson on Thanksgiving when I showed up at the lodge in old sweatpants, not expecting to run into Leo. I might only have a few minutes left, but I was going to look hot the whole time.

No more Old Sage. New Sage planned to resurrect the epic power move from its watery grave and strut past Leo like he was invisible. Assuming he showed up before the clock ran out.

"I can't stay. I have plans. But everything looks perfect. You did a great job."

Valerie blushed and waved away the compliment. "I followed your notes. I'm a huge fan—" She coughed lightly into her fist. "I mean, I'm a huge fan of your ideas."

"Thanks. I'm glad we could work together. You make a great accomplice. Let's stay in touch after I head back to the city."

"I would love that!" Valerie beamed as she pressed her fingers to her earpiece again. She listened intently, then sighed. "Sorry, I have to go. Your dad needs me in the kitchen. There's a beef Wellington emergency. Whatever that means. But let's get drinks before you leave town."

"Count me in." I gave her a quick hug before she hurried toward the back of the house.

Guests had arrived, filling the room with lively conversation and laughter. Soft jazz played in the background, and the scent of cinnamon mingling with vanilla, and the sweetness of freshly baked cookies floated in the air. I made a final pass of the room, greeting people and sharing plans for the holiday, before ending my tour next to the ten-foot Christmas tree.

A bittersweet ache tightened like a ribbon around my heart. This event was a success, and the town had accepted Leo as one of their own. But the funny thing was, they had also accepted me.

I'd become so wrapped up trying to meet everyone's expectations, and hiding the fact I wasn't Agent of the Year, I never noticed when people stopped caring. That sounded harsh, but it was profound. The excitement had lasted a week or two, then faded as it should, in the face of other meaningful moments.

I shouldn't have let it hold so much power. Winning an award would have been an accolade to put on my resume. A hunk of glass to collect dust on a shelf. It didn't define me, and it didn't determine whether I was worthy. Only the way I felt about myself did.

Maybe coming home was about finally letting go of the past and my need to prove myself. Because at the end of the day, I was the only one keeping score.

Too bad my brilliant breakthrough wasn't enough to stop the snow. It still fell, without end, outside the giant picture windows.

I think my curse had glitched, or I was trapped in an evil elf's snow globe. If learning to accept myself wasn't the final answer, then this was one screwed-up game, with no cheat codes, and a brutal boss level.

Good thing there were only two minutes left and still no sign of Leo. *Three ghosts of Christmas, here I come. I'll bring the popcorn, you bring the spooky epiphanies.* Maybe I'd figure out the snow curse through film osmosis.

"That's some dress." The smooth sound of Leo's voice made me jolt. My gaze darted around the room, but I didn't see him. Taking a step forward, I leaned around the Christmas tree and found him holding up the wall.

He wore a dark suit and an even darker expression as his eyes roamed over me.

"Have you been there the whole time? What are you doing hiding behind the Christmas tree?"

"I was watching you. I didn't think you'd come."

I rounded the tree to face him and injected an unhealthy amount of sarcasm in my tone. "I like to finish what I started. I don't discard people just because I achieve my agenda."

One more minute, then I'd walk.

"You think you know everything about me," he muttered. "The truth would shock you."

He pushed away from the wall, stalking closer until he towered over me, and I had to tilt my head to hold his gaze.

"Are you wearing that dress to drive me crazy?" His fingers slid across my hip, thumb caressing the soft velvet. "Because it's working."

A rush of heat joined the venom in my veins. "Good. I'd hate to think you weren't attracted to me, that you kiss every girl you bring up to your private overlook."

His hand flexed, tensing around my waist. I'd hit a nerve.

My time was up. But I didn't move. Every second that ticked by made the party around us grow hazier. The music faded—or maybe it screeched to a halt like a scratched record. I couldn't hear anything over the hammering in my chest.

"Hey, Sage! Leo!" The sound of our names startled me out of my trance. Mrs. Avery stood near one of the banquet tables, pointing to a spot above our heads. "Look. The two of you are under the mistletoe." She gestured to Leo with an encouraging smile. "Go ahead, kiss her."

Looking up, I spotted the infernal plant hanging from the top of the window. I would have laughed at the irony if Leo's interest hadn't dropped to my mouth and lingered there. His hand still claimed my hip, and with the barest tug, I fell against him, his suit jacket brushing against my collarbone.

The air lodged in my throat. I cursed myself for wanting to go through with it, telling my love-starved brain the bliss would outweigh the heartbreak. *Just one more kiss.*

People had stopped to watch, waiting until Leo made his move. But as indecision flipped to a risky resolution in his gaze, I knew I couldn't go through with it.

I sliced a finger through the air, casting a bolt of magic, and held out my palm. The mistletoe snapped from its string and fell into my hand. With a hardened smile, I stuffed it into his jacket pocket and spun on my heel.

Leo's fingers wrapped around my wrist, stopping me from running away. I still had my back to him as he leaned over me, his mouth skimming my ear.

"Well played." His voice dropped low, becoming thick. "Merry Christmas, Bennett."

Leo's touch fell away. I drew in an aching breath, feeling the weight of other people's stares. That was about as close to an epic power move as I could have hoped for, and when I looked over my shoulder, Leo was gone.

I stayed a few minutes more, putting on a brave face, then slipped out into the night. The snow fell softly and the icy air was invigorating. I indulged in it, letting it cool my head. On paper, my mistletoe rejection was a success, but it left me feeling unsteady. Leo's raw sincerity as he wished me Merry Christmas rattled the glass shards in my heart.

Huddling inside my jacket, I waited for my ride, and then asked the driver to drop me off a few blocks from home. I needed to walk. My emotions were too fresh to settle in for a movie.

My heels clicked over the cobblestone; the sound echoing through the quiet street. I passed shops and homes closed and dark for the night; their lit Christmas decorations were a fake sign of life.

I found myself lost on the streets where I'd spent half of my life. The familiar surroundings appeared warped as if I were viewing things through a carnival mirror. I didn't know what to do or what I wanted next. Thanks to my weather curse, I felt snowed in, stuck somewhere between the life I'd worked toward, and the one I had secretly wished to resume. Now neither seemed available to me.

The glow from a colorful fluorescent light caught my attention, and I paused on the sidewalk, not recognizing the shop. Peering through the frost-covered window, I spotted a woman sitting alone at a table. She shuffled a deck of cards, then dealt them one at a time in a tarot reading.

My hand hovered over the doorknob as I debated if my life was really such a disaster that I needed to visit another fortune teller. Delia would be proud. She'd also never let me live it down. But she wasn't here, and I'd run through all my options. Time to consider a dose of mystical wisdom before we were all buried in ice and snow like woolly mammoths in the last Ice Age.

I pushed open the shop door and walked through a silken curtain. The woman collected her cards and gestured to the empty chair at the table like she'd predicted my arrival. She extended her hand after I sat, rings clinking together as we shook.

"My name is Marcy. Welcome to my shop. What brings you here tonight?"

"Guidance?" I said, elongating the word and framing it as a question instead of a request.

Marcy smiled faintly and fanned the deck into an arch. "Pick a card."

I studied them carefully, trying to determine which one would give me the best reading. The last thing I needed to do was draw The Death card. With my luck, the reading would say: *The unlucky witch traveled home on a forced vacation to stop her weather curse. She learned to accept herself. And then, she died.*

"That one." I tapped a card in the middle and slid it out of the spread.

Marcy flipped it over and studied the card. Candles flickered, casting shadows over her face. Her brow creased, and foreboding trickled through my senses. Was there a card worse than death?

"This is The Moon card. It's the card of secrets, illusions, and emotions buried beneath the surface. You'll need to trust your instincts even though everything you've seen before makes you question the truth."

Marcy gripped my hand and her lips parted as a tremor of something undefinable passed between us. "A storm is coming, and you can't run from it."

Her words sent an icy chill down my back. It was the same thing Delia's fortune teller said before the agency party.

I exhaled a shaky laugh. "Have you looked outside lately? The storm's already here."

Marcy squeezed my fingers, then let go, and swept the cards back into a full deck. "The snow doesn't mean you harm. It's trying to lead. What you do with the revelations when you get there is up to you."

Chapter 15
Sage

"This is it, folks! Merry Christmas Eve. Get ready to hunker down because this storm is shaping up to be a snowmageddon. Expect blizzard-like conditions later today. Stay tuned for the full holiday forecast."

I groaned as the radio announcer's voice blared from the alarm clock next to my bed. Who set that thing for seven a.m.? A better question—who set it all? I flopped onto my back, glaring at the blond band leader on my ceiling.

"If I find out it was you, the poster's coming down," I threatened as I kicked off the covers and shuffled toward the window.

Dark clouds gathered overhead, promising the snowpocalypse and the wind whistled through the barren trees. The neighbor across the street was already out salting his porch steps, and a snowplow barreled through, leaving a heavy stream of road salt in its wake.

"Talk about a white Christmas. This is overkill," I grumbled, puttering into the bathroom for a quick shower. After I dried my hair, I wriggled into a pair of black leggings and threw on an oversized cranberry-red sweater before heading downstairs.

A pot of coffee greeted me, but no one else did. The house was eerily quiet. A note on the fridge revealed my parents were next door in the tea shop, and they'd be back soon.

I needed a distraction. Marcy's tarot reading from the other night still rattled in my mind, and I couldn't help but glance outside as the snow started to fall and wonder if this was the 'storm' in question. The radio announcer certainly made it seem like this was the end of days, and if my weather curse was supposed to lead me somewhere, it had better hustle before they shut down the roads.

The presents were wrapped, and the stockings were hung. There wasn't much left to do, so I settled for a little pre-holiday baking. If we lost power, I wanted an army of gingerbread men to keep me company through the dark and stormy night. Waking up single and alone on Christmas morning wouldn't be so bad with a man made of sugar by my side.

My phone jingled, and I licked icing from my fingers before checking the message. It was an email from the agency, informing me Delia had completed her first case. I read through the report, my eyebrows lifting from the unusual mix-up. But Delia had pulled through and earned her promotion—and a little holiday romance on the side. Lucky girl, she'd cut down two Christmas trees with one saw.

"Way to go, Del!" I fist-pumped the air, then tossed a green gumdrop into my mouth in celebration. While the last batch of cookies cooled, I forwarded her the memo, along with my own congratulations. At least Delia's story had a happy ending. Mine had rapidly deteriorated like the weather conditions wreaking havoc outside.

I had finished cleaning the kitchen when my phone jingled again. Tossing the dishrag over the edge of the sink, I grabbed a cookie, excited for Delia's reply.

A scowl formed as I read the message.

Valerie: *Hey Sage, Leo wants his trophy back. Can you swing it by the lodge before the storm hits?*

I scoffed and typed a reply.

Sage: *Tell Mr. Grayson, he can eat snow.*

My phone jingled at Valerie's quick reply.

Valerie: *He's very insistent.*

Sage: *I'll leave it in the mailbox. If he wants it that bad, he can come get it himself.*

My teeth ground together as I pushed off the kitchen stool and stomped up the stairs to my bedroom. That man was unbelievable. I should toss his trophy out the window and let him go scavenger hunting for it in the snowdrifts. Better yet, mail the stupid thing to the North Pole and send him a vague map.

Stuffing the gingerbread cookie in my mouth, I whipped open my closet door and yanked the extra blankets off the trophy. The blanket knocked over a box stacked next to the pile, spilling the contents onto the carpet. Folders and files labeled with the tea shop emblem were scattered at my feet. My parents must have used my bedroom closet for extra storage.

I kneeled and collected the papers, trying to organize them as best as I could before placing them back in the box. One document made me pause for a second look, and I flipped through the sheets of paper, unease coiling in my stomach.

They were the loan papers my parents had signed to repair the tea shop a few months before I left town. I scanned the signature lines; the unease tightening into full-blown disgust. Leo's father had issued them the loan. He'd nearly bankrupted them, and destroyed the tea shop just like he'd destroyed other areas of town.

My heartbeat pounded in my ears, hands shaking as I sifted through the other papers on the floor. I found a canceled check, my mind reeling as I read the signature line. It was from Leo. He'd written a check to my dad for almost twenty thousand dollars. I checked the date and realized he'd issued it eight months ago.

What was going on? Why would Leo write a check to my parents after he returned to Cold Spell? It couldn't be an advance for their events at the lodge. It was too much money.

I felt sick. Gathering the forms and the canceled check, I ran downstairs, stuffed my feet into a pair of boots, and rushed over to the tea shop.

My dad looked up as I burst through the swinging kitchen door. His brow furrowed in concern.

"What's the matter? You look like the cat who knocked over the Christmas tree."

"Very funny. We don't have a cat." I dropped the files onto the counter and jabbed Leo's check. "What is this? Why did

Leo give you money, and how come you never told me his father was the one who held the tea shop loan?"

My dad's features went as white as the flour dusting his palms. He reached for a rag to clean off, his jaw working as he tried to answer.

"Sage, is that you, honey?" My mom poked her head out of the office door.

"Come here, Suzanne. We need to talk with Sage," Dad said, leaning heavily on the counter. He flipped through the documents and sighed. "I'm sorry. Leo never wanted you to find out, and your mom and I agreed with him. But it's too late for that now."

I swallowed around the lump in my throat. "Find out, what, Dad?"

"The truth about what happened before you left. Leo's father discovered the two of you were getting close, and he wasn't happy about it. He expected more from his son than dating the daughter of a family with a history like ours—a lineage filled with witchcraft." Dad shook his head and exhaled a disgruntled sound through his nose. "So Mr. Grayson used his wealth and power to stop it.

"Your mother and I weren't aware at the time of the shady loan conditions when we signed the papers. We were excited to get the repairs done and get back on our feet and assumed everything was legitimate. That was our mistake. We should have paid better attention. But after we signed the papers, Leo's father told his son he would call in the loan early and foreclose on the tea shop unless he stopped seeing you."

"Dad…" Tears burned the corners of my eyes. *That's why Leo never showed up for our date.* I wiped the tears away only to find more fill their place. "When did you find out?"

My dad placed a hand on my shoulder. "After Leo purchased the lodge and returned to Cold Spell. He came to see us at the tea shop. That's when he told us the truth and wrote us a check to replace the money we took from our retirement savings to pay off the dirty loan. Leo felt terrible and blamed himself. He also made us promise you wouldn't find out. He thought knowing the truth was more painful than what happened, and we agreed. Those kids tormented you growing up and we couldn't have you believing you were to blame for a cruel man's prejudice."

I ran both hands over my face, pressing my fingers into my eyelids. I had misunderstood everything and assumed Leo had callously stood me up for our date, and then moved on with someone else the same week. He had refused to see me afterward, and even got himself reassigned to another ski class. But it wasn't because he didn't care, but because he'd made a painful choice.

My mother pulled me into a hug, smoothing her hand down the back of my hair. "Shh. It's okay. You didn't do anything wrong. We love you exactly as you are."

I blinked over her shoulder, spotting the wall of embellished photos. So many secrets and hidden truths. Look where they had gotten me.

"Mom," I sniffed. "I never won Agent of the Year. I only said I did because I didn't want to let either of you down."

Mom drew back and brushed the hair out of my eyes. "There's always next year, sweetie."

A strangled laugh burst from my throat, and Dad coughed to hide his amusement. *Some things will never change.*

"Yeah, maybe. Right now I'm happy with the way things are. I'm glad I helped with the rink project. An award wouldn't have changed that. And hardly anyone even talks about it anymore. It was stupid to be so obsessed with it. But I wanted you guys to know the truth."

"We are proud of you either way, and we are so happy you're home to celebrate Christmas with us this year." My mother looked over at my dad and frowned. "We should tell her the rest, David."

"There's more?"

My dad picked up Leo's check and stared at it, then smiled. "We never blamed Leo for what happened. That boy cares about you a lot. So I only used half of his money to pay back our savings. We'll catch up thanks to the tea events we're hosting at the lodge. The rest of his money, I gave back to him—or at least, I did anonymously to help fund the rink project."

"You're the donor?" I asked.

"We felt it was the right thing to do," Mom added. "Well, now that everything is out in the open, we should close up and head back to the house before this storm gets any worse."

The storm. Marcy's words replayed in my mind. I knew what I had to do. No more running away. Not when I could run toward the person, I wanted most. If Leo pushed me away again, it might make for an awkward Christmas Eve, but holiday miracles didn't come without risk. I'd waited years for mine, and I wasn't leaving until I got it.

"I have to go to the lodge. I need to see Leo."

My mother pointed toward the window. "Right now? But it's already started to snow."

"I'm taking the car. If I hurry, I can get there before the roads close. It's not far."

"Let her go, Suzanne." Dad gave me a quick hug and planted a kiss on the top of my head. "Text us when you get there so we know you made it safely."

"But what about Christmas?" Mom said. "You might get stuck at the lodge."

A warm feeling expanded inside my chest. "I'm counting on it."

The windshield wipers couldn't keep up with the snow. Huge flakes stuck to the glass, making it nearly impossible to see. I gripped the steering wheel, easing the car over the icy road. Only a little farther. Five more minutes and I'd be parked at the lodge.

There were no other cars on the road. Everyone else was sensibly tucked away in their homes to brave the blizzard. The radio announcer mocked me through the car's speakers with potential snow totals and threats of massive power outages.

But the radio guy wasn't dealing with a weather curse. One where his future happiness hinged on confronting this beast of a storm and coming out the winner.

The car swerved on a patch of ice, and I yelped, turning into the slide. My stomach flipped as the car jerked to a stop, the wheels spinning without traction. I tried again, with no luck, and banged my palm on the steering wheel.

I'd have to walk the rest of the way. The wind roared as I pushed open the car door and slung my bag over my shoulder. My boots sank into the snow up to my calves, and I lurched forward, raising my arm to block the stinging snow from my eyes.

When the lodge came into view, I nearly sank to my knees in relief. I was freezing and probably looked like a yeti lost in a frozen tundra. My cheeks had to be as red as Rudolph's nose, and I was positive there were icicles in my hair. If Leo didn't fall head over heels in love with me the moment he saw me, he had a valid excuse.

I trudged toward the lodge's entrance and pulled on the massive wrought iron handle. The door didn't budge. Cupping my mittened hands around the sides of my face, I peered through the narrow window. It was dark inside. The lobby was empty.

"No!" I moaned, pounding on the door with my fist as if someone would magically appear when the lodge was clearly closed. *This is why you call first before making a grand romantic gesture!*

I sat down on the step and dropped my head into my hands. I was really in a frozen pickle now. My car was in a ditch and I was stuck outside the lodge. I was supposed to be snowed in, not snowed out!

"Sage?" Leo's voice rose over the wind. I hadn't even heard the door open. "What are you doing out here?"

He hauled me up before I could answer. Which was helpful because my teeth were chattering and an explanation might have to wait until I thawed. Off came my hat and my gloves as he pressed his warm hands against my cheeks.

"Are you trying to freeze to death on my front steps?" Leo led me through the dark lobby and into the great room where the fireplace crackled with warmth. He unzipped my coat, tugged my arms out of the sleeves, and wrapped a thick, cozy blanket over my shoulders.

Then he paced; boots hitting the hardwood in front of me. Back and forth while he opened and closed his fists. It was kind of cute in a menacing, protective kind of way.

He stopped short and kneeled in front of me. "Where's your car? I didn't see it in the parking lot. And what were you thinking driving in this?"

I winced. "My parents' car is on the side of the road. I may have spun out and had to walk from the bottom of the hill."

Leo closed his eyes as if he needed all his senses to control himself. When he opened them again, I held up a finger.

"Hold on. You can scold me in a second. I have to send a text." I pulled out my phone and typed a message to my dad. "By the way, where is everyone?"

"The blizzard forecast called for widespread power outages and our backup generator is broken. Valerie was supposed to have a tech out to fix it last week, but she must have forgotten. So with the possibility of long-term power outages, we relocated the guests to another hotel downtown, and I sent everyone else home."

"So it's just us here? All alone? Until the snow stops?"

"Yeah. Just us."

The wind howled against the windows, slamming into the panes like a monster trying to get inside. I shivered, not from the cold, but from the twist of fate.

"Are you warm enough?" Leo murmured.

I wrinkled my nose. "My feet are cold, and I don't think I can transfer enough heat through my frozen fingers to warm them up."

A faint smile curled the edge of Leo's mouth. He helped me slip out of my boots and placed them by the fire, then he joined me on the sofa and allowed me to tuck my sock-covered feet into his lap.

Leo grunted and shifted deeper into the couch. "We'll have to do this the old-fashioned way. I don't want you to get hypothermia or something."

"Yeah. Then we'd have to strip naked so you could save me with your body heat."

I bit the side of my cheek hard to keep from laughing at Leo's choked expression. His gaze darkened, and I couldn't tell if he was imagining that scenario or planning to wring my neck.

"What are you doing here, Bennett?"

I bent over and reached into my bag, pulling out Leo's trophy. "You wanted this back, so here it is."

"You drove through a blizzard to return a stupid hunk of glass? I swear—"

"Fine, you don't want it?" I pulled my feet from his lap. "I'll leave. I'm sure I can push the car back onto the road—"

Leo silenced me with a look and dragged my feet back. "You're staying. I don't care if I have to tie you up with Christmas lights. You don't step a foot out of this lodge until the snow stops and the roads are clear."

"Yes, sir." I sent him a mock salute. "You know," I mused after the silence had trickled in. "I've never been tied up with Christmas lights. Is that another one of your villainous tricks? I might like it."

He hissed out a breath. "You're on very thin ice. Be careful, Bennett."

We listened as the fire snapped and cracked; the only other sound besides the gusty wind. Leo had lit candles, strategically placing them around the room. The flickering glow was soothing and cast deep shadows across Leo's profile. Somehow it made him more captivating like a mystery box with no apparent opening.

My original plan had been to burst through the door and tell him I knew everything. But there was something about this moment and this earthshaking clarity that allowed me to see him fully, while he tried to maintain his guard. It was in those cracks I felt his affection, and maybe something more.

We weren't going anywhere. Not tonight. The snow had been pushing me here to discover the truth, and now that I was standing in its path, I wanted to see everything I'd missed. Leo would not confess. I knew that much. He would have told me at the overlook. Leo was holding onto his secret. Afraid to let it go. I was going to have to draw it out of him.

And maybe have a little fun while doing it.

"So, what should we do to pass the time? It is Christmas Eve. We might as well make the best of an unpleasant situation."

Leo gave me a side-eye glare. "I think you should sit in silence and contemplate your reckless actions. I'm still upset you drove here."

"Yeah, I'm not going to do that." I wriggled my toes against his abdomen, feeling him tense. I lifted a brow in challenge.

"Actually, I was thinking we should play a game."

Chapter 16

Sage

Leo placed the letter tiles onto the board, spelling out the word that got him twelve points on the scorecard.

"Really? You went with, agony? You just played, tormented, and before that—" I glanced at the board. "You played, haunted. I'm sensing a theme. Who are you, Heathcliff from *Wuthering Heights?*"

Leo cocked his head and pressed his mouth into a grimace. "You're the one who wanted to play a board game. I voted for silence."

"If I remember correctly, I suggested we play *Twister*. You're the one who chose *Scrabble.*"

"It was the safer choice," he said under his breath as he pushed off the sofa to throw another log into the fireplace.

It was hotter than a snowman in the Bahamas in here. Leo kept adding logs to the fire every time I got too close. If I even moved within a three-foot radius of him, he was up, stoking the flames like a man possessed.

I took a cool drink from the glass of water on the table, but it did little to tame the heat. I fanned my face and reached for the hem of my sweater.

"What are you doing?" Leo pointed the fire poker in my direction.

"Relax. I'm melting over here. You're taking your job as Fire Master a little too seriously." I pulled the sweater over my head and tossed it over the back of the sofa. Then I patted the cushion. "I'm ready to play my next word."

Leo's gaze roamed over my ice-blue silk camisole. His throat worked, and his chest rose on a deep inhale. Warily, he sat on the sofa. Three feet away.

I placed the tiles one by one, then flashed Leo an innocent smile. "Tempting, six points."

Leo mumbled a curse.

He scrubbed a hand over his jaw and dropped his head back like he was in pain. I almost took pity on the man. Trying to push him over the edge was wrong, and I fully expected a lump of coal in my stocking tomorrow morning, but I was having too much fun to stop.

If you're snowed in with your enemy-turned-potential lover, you take advantage of the situation first.

It's science.

The snow had piled up outside and still fell in a swirl of white as the day faded into night. There was something almost tranquil about watching it through the window; the raging force separated by a barrier of glass and wood.

I'd been running from one thing to the next for so long, it felt good to stop. Facing the storm wasn't only about uncovering secrets. It was about slowing down long enough to appreciate the moments I missed most. The quiet ones by the fire. The long looks. How my heart fluttered by being near someone. A laugh that made my cheeks ache.

It was those simple things that made Leo and me great. Even after all these years. Even after the hurt. We couldn't bury that part of us.

And Leo was trying—poorly. He just hadn't realized yet I had no intention of letting him push me away this time.

The shadows deepened, making the candles glow brighter, the wax pooling inside the glass jars.

I moved closer to Leo, scooting the three feet to lean over him. His head jerked, eyes opening to find me pressed against him.

"Bennett." He whispered my name as if it were an ache he couldn't soothe. He was the only one who'd ever called me that, and hearing it now, filled with such quiet intensity was almost my breaking point.

Slowly, I reached past him to twist my fingers around the candle wick in the jar near his elbow. The extinguished flame ignited back to life on a spark of magic.

"The candle went out," I murmured, as his ragged breath fanned my neck. He'd gone still, a whipcord tightness in his muscles. His hands settled around my waist as if he'd lost the fight battling for control.

He was warm and solid beneath me, and I couldn't hold on to my secret any longer. My game had lost its appeal to the possibility of the real thing. An honest relationship with Leo. My mischief paled in the face of that.

My lips parted; the words on the edge of my tongue.

Leo made a rough sound in the back of his throat as he lifted me off him. I bounced on the couch cushion, staring at the spot Leo had been.

He was up again, this time pacing in front of the windows. Tension radiated from him, and I stood, wiping anxious palms down my leggings. I might have gone too far with that one.

I was lucky Leo hadn't tossed me in a snowbank. I had it coming.

"Okay, so maybe no more board games. We could try something more cerebral. How about Two Truths and a Lie? I'll start."

Leo spun toward me, his expression as fierce as the storm raging beyond the window. His humorless laugh echoed into the rafters.

"Enough, Sage. I don't know if this is some twisted version of revenge, and maybe I deserve it, but I've had enough."

He prowled closer, and I stepped back until I bumped the edge of the sofa. There was nowhere else to go.

To answer my earlier question about walking in nature, yes, there were bears in Cold Spell. I just poked one, and now I had to stay still, hoping he wouldn't devour me whole.

Leo's body pinned me in place, and a strange note burned in his voice when he spoke.

"No more fireside games. No more leaning over me, wearing nothing but silk." His finger deliberately trailed along the thin strap of my camisole, making my stomach clench. "And most of all—" Leo grasped my chin, tilting my head until our gazes locked. "Stop making my only Christmas Eve with you a brutal reminder of what I lose when the snow stops."

Leo's words sucked all the air out of the room. Even the wind obeyed, smothering its wicked howl. The silence had a weight to it, making my chest constrict until I swallowed a breath, my voice wavering when I spoke.

"I said, I'll start. Two Truths and a Lie."

Leo's gaze grew cold, giving the ice outside a run for its money, but I kept going. He was right. I'd had enough too.

"One: you taught me how to ski. Two: I won Agent of the Year. And three: Your father threatened to ruin my parents unless you stopped seeing me. So you stayed away and never showed up for our date."

"What?" Leo asked.

He searched my face as if something there could lessen the shot I launched across the bow. But it hit him square in the chest; staggering and fatal. The fight leached out of him, replaced by a searing fear. He gripped my arms, tightening until his hands stopped shaking.

"Bennett, I can explain—"

"Which one is the lie?"

"The second one." His tone was flat, almost deadened.

"And when you pushed me away on the overlook, you did it because you thought I'd eventually find out what happened and hate you for it?"

Leo swallowed hard. "Truth"

"But you were wrong. I'm not angry. Not at you. I'm furious at your father for making you choose. How cruel."

My hand cupped the side of Leo's face, and he leaned into it.

I steadied my voice. "I'm touched you offered to pay back my parents and help them get ahead, and while I was infatuated with the boy who taught me to ski, I am in love with the man who bought this lodge and blackmailed me into helping him save it."

"That better be another truth," Leo said, his voice rough with emotion.

"It is."

"I love you, Bennett," Leo whispered into my mouth as he pulled me in for a lingering kiss. He dragged himself away with a groan and pressed our foreheads together.

"I have loved you since I first saw you warm up your boots. I tried to stop, and I know I broke your heart, but I have loved you every day. Every minute. And every second you didn't know that, kills me. Because you need to know how much you mean to me. How much I want to spend every single Christmas with you. Every holiday. Every day."

I poked him in the chest with a soft laugh. "Well, I work holidays."

"Then I go to where you are."

"It's a deal," I said, going up on my toes to seal it with a kiss.

Leo framed my face with his hands, and we sank onto the sofa. He deepened the kiss. The feel of his mouth was almost too addictive, rivaling the heated moment at the overlook.

But this time, it didn't end the same way.

We didn't rush. The snow was the perfect accomplice. A card-carrying member of Team Villain savoring its nefarious scheme.

It deserved a promotion.

I wrapped my legs around Leo's waist as his mouth trailed kisses along my collarbone, my head falling back with a silent moan. Heat from the fireplace warmed my back, and the quiet crackle of the flames were hypnotic as I slid my hands into his hair.

"It's always been you, Bennett," Leo's husky murmur, had me searching for his mouth again. He kissed me with those words still hanging in the air, until they became part of me. Until I believed it.

He gentled the kiss, almost reluctant to pull away, but when I searched his face, I understood the look in his eyes. We had all night, and maybe there was even a small part of him afraid I'd be gone by morning. But I wasn't going anywhere. This was where I belonged.

Leo wrapped his arms around me as we lay on the sofa. The quiet settled around us in the place where we'd met. The place Leo had restored with his own hand, and the place where our hearts felt most at home.

"I can't believe you're mine this Christmas," he said, tracing light circles over my skin with the tips of his fingers.

I snuggled deeper in his arms. "I can't believe you wore an elf costume."

Leo winced. "I can't believe a photo of it ran in the paper."

"I kept it, you know."

"So did I." He tickled my ribs. "We'll have to print a copy for your parents' collage of awkward Sage photos."

"Watch it. You're about to be featured prominently and often on that wall. I'd consider a haircut."

Leo gasped teasingly and pressed the palm of my hand to his lips. "I'll have you know, this haircut scored me a two-year contract with a winter sportswear catalog. The sweater I wore had rave reviews, and it wasn't because of the fiber count."

"My apologies to your adoring fans."

"Don't apologize to yourself. I forgive you."

My grin widened as Leo tilted my chin up to chase it away with his mouth.

"I think the snow stopped," I said. I glanced out the window, feeling a beautiful peace fill my heart. My snow curse was broken. The wind had stilled, the clouds parting to reveal a bright moon. A blanket of snow glistened under its light.

Leo didn't even bother to look. "No, it didn't. You're officially snowed in until I say otherwise. We might be here for days. Weeks."

"A month at least. It was a terrible storm."

"Dreadful. We may never dig ourselves out."

I pressed another kiss to his lips. "It's almost midnight. Merry Christmas, Grayson."

"Merry Christmas, Bennett."

Epilogue

Leo

"Have I ever told you how much I love this mattress?" Sage stretched like a cat, and I pulled her closer, nuzzling my face into her neck. Our feet tangled together, my body wrapped around hers. I was a man obsessed.

"You have. I remember it vividly. Among other things."

Sage chuckled and ran her fingers through my disheveled hair. "Well, as much as I adore it, and have plans to return pretty much exclusively, we can't stay in it all day. It's Christmas, and we have plans."

"Plans to shovel? Because one of your magical storms basically shut down Cold Spell. Sorry, sweetheart, Christmas is cance—"

Her hand slapped over my mouth. "Don't *ever* say those words. And don't *ever* underestimate the magic of Christmas."

Never again. It was impossible not to believe after I'd received everything I'd ever wanted this year. And the greatest gift of all was the incredible woman lying in my arms. I'd never look at snow the same way again. Every flake, every storm would remind me of her. Luckily, I owned a ski resort.

Sage rolled out of bed and shuffled to the window. She pulled back the heavy curtain and waved her arms like she was unveiling the world's most elaborate ice sculpture.

"See. That's the fun of mystical blizzards. All the snow. None of the cleanup. The roads are clear and the power's back on. Get dressed. We're having lunch with my parents."

I should grieve the end of our snowed-in experience, and a part of me wanted to close the curtain and pretend, but I'd never had a true family Christmas before. While the Bennetts had their quirks, they cared about each other. If I was given the chance to earn even a little of that, not even a mountain of snow would keep me away.

"Do you think your dad will teach me how to make his famous quiche?" I asked over my shoulder as I turned the handle on the shower.

Sage poked her head into the bathroom. "Be careful what you wish for. My dad will be so excited you want to learn, the two of you will be wearing matching 'kiss the cook' aprons next Christmas."

"Is that a promise? Because I'm my most attractive while wearing an apron with a witty catchphrase."

"Not according to my spell book. Less is more." Sage winked, and somehow, I fell even a little more in love with her.

After a quick shower and calls to the staff, wishing them a happy holiday with orders to stay home and enjoy a few days off, Sage and I walked through the empty lobby on our way to her parent's house.

Sage slowed as she approached the counter, finding a white envelope with a strange logo stamped on the outside.

"That wasn't there last night, was it?" she asked, lifting the envelope and turning it over to study the emblem.

"No. Who's it from?" I peered over her shoulder as she warily removed the folded parchment.

From the Desk of Valerie Spellman
Hey guys! Merry Christmas.

Sorry, I can't be there to celebrate. From one agent to another, there's nothing better than getting to revel in the afterglow of a holiday miracle. Especially one as magical as yours. Though you guys kept me on my toes.

Sage, I am your biggest fan and modeled my casework after yours. Minus the Fourth of July incident—it shall henceforth never be mentioned again—but you're my inspiration.

I hope we can officially work together someday, and if not soon, then save me a spot in the Conga line at the next kickoff party. I hear you have some pretty sweet dance moves.

And Leo, best boss ever. Sorry, you have to find another assistant. I will miss being your festive minion.

P.S. My bad for disabling the backup generator. It's not broken. Just reconnect the battery. But I hope you found other ways to keep warm.

Take care!
Valerie

"Did I read that right?" I shook my head, trying to make sense of Valerie's letter. "Does she work with you?"

Sage laughed and pressed the letter to her heart. "It seems so. We're tricky witches and show up where you least expect. But we're always there, working behind the scenes."

I wrapped my arms around Sage's shoulders and kissed the top of her head. "Us regular folks are just fortunate to have you." My brow creased. "By the way, what's the Fourth of July incident?"

Sage tensed. She turned in my arms, her bottom lip bending under the crush of her teeth. After a few seconds of indecision, she patted my chest and huffed a breath.

"All right, Grayson. Let's go get my parents' car. I'll tell you on the way. But if you even think about telling anyone, I'll have to silence you and tie you up with Christmas lights."

I chuckled under my breath and leaned forward to whisper in her ear, "That's not the threat you think it is, Bennett."

Her eyes narrowed. "Only a villain would say that."

My fingers interlaced with hers as I tugged her toward the door. "You keep my secret, and I'll keep yours."

Books Also by
Jenna Collett

Witching You Series
Witching You A Charmed Christmas
Witching You Weren't Snowed In

Ever Dark, Ever Deadly Series
Spellbound After Midnight
Wolfish Charms
Stranded and Spellbound
Shatter the Dark
Edge of Wonder

Made in United States
North Haven, CT
28 November 2024